Deeper

IN YOU

THE PHOENIX SERIES BOOK 2

The Phoenix Series:
Deep in You
Deeper in You

BROKEN HEARTS STILL BEAT

Deeper
IN YOU

THE PHOENIX SERIES BOOK 2

DAVID S. SCOTT

Printed in the United States of America

First Printing: July 2016

Published by Seraph Wing Publishing

ISBN-13 978-0-9907111-7-9 (ebook)

ISBN-13 978-0-9907111-9-3 (print)

ACKNOWLEDGEMENTS:

A huge thank you to my incredible wife, Stephanie. Your love and support mean so much to me. Most of this story would not have been possible without your encouragement and faith.

To my personal assistant (PitA), Melissa Ann, how you put up with my nonsense (I was going to use a different word but was told it was bad to curse in acknowledgments) each day is beyond me. Yet here you are, making me write, organizing the street team, and tirelessly promoting and supporting me. You've been with me since the start of this crazy adventure, back when Xander was a tantra instructor. My how things changed. But you stayed with me, encouraging me and guiding me. I can't ever thank you enough.

I'd like to thank my editor, Matt Schiariti, for all your help and ideas. You may have made me wonder if I even know *how* to speak English, but the book wouldn't be anywhere near as good without you so I'm glad to have endured the torture.

A special thanks to the very talented Darkmantle Designs for the wonderful job on the cover and formatting.

To all the members of my street team, David's Decadent Divas, I appreciate everything you do. You ladies promote every day, and have done so even before my books were even close to being released. If it weren't for you, no one would have ever heard of me or my books. Thank you so much for everything.

To my Beta Readers—Melissa Ann, Ella Medler, Elizabeth Booth Bennett, Lacia Carabas, Marcia Mason-Heaston, Tammy Markowski, Terrie Meerschaert, Rachelle Pianalto Jones, Cristiane Karamanolis, Denise Williams, Tosha Merritt Rabideau, Kathy Atwell, Chrisstine Hague Pearce, and Donna Tripi Salzano—thank you for everything you have done. Each and every one of you has touched this book in some way, and helped to make it better.

Last, but not least, a huge thanks to you, the reader. Without readers, there would be no reason for writers to write. I hope you enjoy *Deeper in You* and consider leaving a review to let me and other readers know what you thought about this book.

This book is dedicated to everyone that stuck with me over the last year, "patiently" waiting for Xander's story to be released. Yes, all of you that attended my takeovers, sent me messages, and generally nagged me for release dates. Now that it's finally finished, I hope you consider the wait to be worth it. To all of you, I have one question to ask:

Do you believe in fate?

TABLE OF CONTENTS

CHAPTER ONE

"Lily Campbell, will you do me the honor of being my wife?"

The situation was far from ideal. I was proposing to a woman I barely knew, my career was over, and my back was broken. I'm not sure how much more fucked up this situation could be, but I was determined to make the best of it and get our lives back on track. Lily was pregnant with my child, and I knew we could be happy together, knew that we had to try. Perhaps I hadn't done such a great job of showing her how supportive I could be before, but it should be obvious now. I'd brought her a bouquet of roses and lilies. I'd picked out her ring, a stunning two-karat princess cut which had set me back quite a bit. I looked at her, hoping my feelings shone through my eyes and smile.

She dropped the flowers on the floor, causing some of them to spill out of the green cellophane wrapping. The chaotic way the fragile buds splayed on the floor reflected my frayed nerves. I forced myself to look at her face, noticing the blood had drained away, leaving her as pale as the white sand

Florida beaches were famous for. Her mouth hung open. If the situation hadn't been so serious, her expression would have been comical—a perfect caricature of shock.

I waited for her to pull herself together. I knew my question had come as a surprise, but this was the right thing to do. I'd stay by her side and we'd raise our baby together.

Finally, her mouth closed, and color returned to her cheeks. She seemed to have gained back some of her composure. I waited patiently for her to accept and put me out of my misery.

"Oh, Xander… no."

I swallowed. "N-no?" My breathing was erratic. I felt confused, and my head swam as I tried to make sense of what she said.

"No. I'm sorry. I can't. I–I have to go." She fled past me and out the door before I could manage to form another thought.

A pain worse than what trampled my spine and shoulder tore through my chest. What did this mean? She couldn't possibly intend to raise the baby by herself, could she? Had I screwed up that badly? I hobbled into my kitchen and grabbed a shot glass, filling it with three fingers of Patrón. I wasn't sure if it would be the pain in my chest or my injuries that would do me in. I slammed the drink back and stared at the front door, a tiny crack letting in the humid Orlando air. Should I call her? The questions circled around my brain, and I had trouble grasping any single one of them.

No. I'd call her later. Let her have tonight to calm down. I was certain she'd be back when she had time to process everything. I'd needed time to process things, too.

Damn. Pregnant women and their hormones, I poured another glass of tequila and took a big sip. Would it really be so bad if we didn't get married? We could still get along like reasonable adults and take care of our son or daughter, even if we ended up apart. I downed the rest of the shot and poured a third.

Why the hell would she tell me no, anyway? I took a long swallow of the smooth liquor and frowned. I'd offered her everything I am and would be with that ring. I was good looking, and charming, and… why would she just toss me aside? Fuck her.

Standing in my kitchen, drinking alone, it struck me how much of a loser I was. I grabbed the bottle of Patrón and hobbled to the living room to ease myself onto the couch, shutting the front door as I passed. This was much better… now I was sitting in the living room drinking alone. Much more suave.

I pulled out my phone and took a swig straight from the bottle. I should call her. What would I say? No, I couldn't. I shouldn't. She'd run out on *me*, not the other way around. My chest still hurt. Damn it.

I sat on the couch, drinking and staring at my phone. I lost all sense of time; I could have been sitting there for hours for all I knew. The previously full bottle was about to run dry, I needed… needed…

Fuck. I was gonna hurl.

I rose to my feet and stumbled, nearly falling. My back throbbed as I jerked to remain on my feet. In a split-second decision, I painfully stumbled toward the kitchen.

I violently emptied the contents of my stomach into the garbage can, then slumped to the floor. My phone had fallen near the couch. I crawled toward it. The room spun. My vision blurred. I grabbed the wretched device and shakily pressed the icon with Lily's picture. The sound of ringing filled my ears.

"What, Xander?" she snapped.

"We have to talk," I slurred.

"We have nothing to talk about and I'm busy now."

"Bisshy? You need to make time for me, becaush–"

"Are you drunk? What the hell is the matter with you? I thought you'd be happy. Look, Xander, we had some fun times, had some laughs, but we both knew this wasn't going anywhere. Look how you panicked at the first sign of trouble. I have no idea what possessed you to pull that stunt with the ring, but we weren't there yet. To be honest, I'm not sure we were ever going to be there, but now I know we never will. You've ruined it."

"Lily, shtop. Shtop. We can talk thish out—"

I forced myself to get up and limp to the kitchen counter. I needed to focus. I was so determined to get there I almost missed what she was saying. Almost… but not quite.

"No, we can't talk this out. I have to go. I don't want to see you again, and won't be hitting you up for child support because there will be no child. I've made an appointment at the clinic. Leave me alone."

"Y-you… you made an appointment? When? Why? I thought you shaid you loved me…"

"Clearly, I was wrong to think that. You're nothing but an immature adolescent yourself. How could we possibly handle a baby? Anyway, I don't want any kids. Not with you, not with anyone. Not now, maybe not ever. I made the appointment yesterday, after I woke up here alone. After you walked out on me. I spent the rest of the day moving my stuff out. You only caught me there this morning because I'd forgotten something."

"Lily, please don't... Don't do this. Don't get an abortion. We can work this out. If you don't want to raise our baby, then I will. Please. Lily, I'll get on my knees and beg." I struggled to coherently form the words. This was too important for there to be any misunderstanding. life was too short, too precious. The loss of my sister had taught me that. Combine that with my failed career, and it was just one more thing to be stripped away from me. I had nothing left to lose.

Silence was my only response. I looked at my phone. She'd hung up.

I reached for a bottle of Bacardi 151, took a long draw, then scrolled through phone numbers until I found Sam Henderson's entry. My coach was probably the closest thing I had to a best friend. I punched it without thinking. It went straight to voicemail.

"Sam, Xander. Lishten, Lily said no. She's ending everything, so no kid. Want to come over and get shmashed with me? Call me back or just drop by." There. I sounded calm, cool, and collected. I think.

I couldn't believe she was going to have an abortion. Why? How could she do this to me? To us? I drank some more, using what strength of will I had left to make sure it stayed down. Where did…

My eyes rolled back in my head as a ringing filled my ears. What was I thinking? It was… where…

CHAPTER TWO

An insistent pounding in my head roused me. I covered my eyes with my palms and tried to block it out, only to realize the sound was coming from the door. Not only that, but my phone was buzzing as well.

"Xander!" *Knock. Knock. Knock.* "Xander! Open up, already."

Sam sounded pissed about something.

I tried to sit up, but agony coursed through me like fire. My stomach churned, and I submitted to my body's demands and remained on the floor. The carpeting reeked of Bacardi and vomit, but I was too miserable to care.

The volume increased. It almost felt like Sam was knocking directly on my head. He clearly wasn't going to go away any time soon. I struggled to think. I had shut that door, but had I locked it?

"It's open," I rasped. The sound that emerged from my throat was not my own. Rather, it sounded like a demonic frog with laryngitis.

The banging continued unabated. He couldn't hear me. Summoning the last of my strength, I snatched the phone up and answered it with the speaker button. No need to look at who was calling. "What?"

"What the fuck is wrong with you? Answer this damn door."

I dropped the phone, wincing, and closed my eyes to block out the influx of agony at the sound.

"Xander…?"

"Did you try the knob?" I muttered.

"What was that?"

"I said… the God damned door was never locked, asshole. Turn the knob."

Sam walked in, the bright Florida sunlight painful even through my closed eyelids. I squirmed, fighting the pain in order to turn my head away.

"What have you done?" Sam's judgmental tone broke through my bubble of self-pity as I heard him drop onto the couch.

"Got drunk. The hell does it look like?"

"I could tell *that* from your message. Xander… you should see yourself."

"Fuck off."

"No. I get that you're going through a shit time right now. But you know what? You're not the first guy to ever knock up a girl. You were careless and you fucked up. Worse, you allowed it to control you so much that you've completely screwed up the rest of your life."

"You think I don't know that?" I tried to sit up, but surrendered once more to gravity and settled back on the wet carpet. "I've lost everything. My life has gone downhill since the day I met her. First the drugs, then the baby. She's been screwing with my mind and my emotions since day one."

"That's enough. You're going to listen to me and you're going to listen hard. I don't know what sort of friendship you think we have, but let me spell it out for you. I am your coach. That is first and foremost. I am also your friend and sometimes—unfortunately—your confidant. I've known you forever, and let me tell you, this is not you. You've become a pussy. My, how the mighty have fallen, Xander. You need to decide: you can either get your shit together, learn to take responsibility for your own choices, and fight to reclaim the man you once were. Or... you can wallow here like a lovesick teenager, blaming Lily and bad luck and generally acting like the pussy you are. Either way, you need to remember that I am your coach and I will not come over here, watch you drink yourself stupid, and be cool with it. Got me?"

"Sorry I called. Sorry I was mistaken that you were my friend. But I'm not sure what I need a coach for anymore. I'm done. Washed up."

"You keep going like this, you will be. And I *am* your friend, asswipe."

"Just leave me alone. I'm fine."

"You are not fucking fine. You can't even get up, can you?"

Silence was my answer.

"That floor looks disgusting and, frankly, it reeks in here."

"Then go away."

"How's the back?"

"How the hell do you think? It's broken, God damn it."

"Have you been taking your pills?"

Pills... where did I leave those? "No. Not even sure where they are."

Sam heaved a big sigh and stood. "Come on, hotshot. Let's get you off the floor. I can't stay long. My wife was almost done cooking dinner when I noticed your message. I scared the shit out of her."

Strong arms gripped my chest, under my arms, and lifted. Too tired to either fight or help, I just let him pull me up into a kneeling position, and assist me to my feet.

"Hurts, Sam. It all hurts."

"I know, kid. Bed or couch?"

"Couch, I guess. Stairs don't sound fun."

"No, you'll need to get your stuff moved down for a while. I can call John and we'll come help tomorrow."

"It's cool. Only thing I need from there is clothes. I'll go up once and throw everything over the landing or some shit. It's no big deal. I don't need help."

"Xander–"

"Just leave me the fuck alone for a while, Sam. Okay? I don't want help."

"Fine. You should eat, though."

I glared at him. "I'm not eating jack shit. In case you haven't noticed by my sunny disposition, I'm fighting a hangover. Know what sucks? Drunk puking. Know what's worse than that? Drunk puking with a broken back."

"You did it to yourself."

"Thanks. That really helps."

"Glad to hear it does. You should remember what I said."

A grunt was my only response. I knew Sam meant well, but I wanted him and his noise to get out of my house. I never should have told him he could come in.

"All right." Sam walked into my kitchen and returned a moment later to press a cold water bottle into my hands. "Drink some water, at least. Where are your pain pills?"

I closed my eyes. When I got home, I'd called to Lily, proposed, then started drinking. Had to be either here or in the car. I shifted in my seat and pulled my prescription bottle out of my pocket.

"Good. You should take one. You heard the doctor: you'll heal faster if you stay ahead of the pain instead of chasing it. That way, your body can focus on getting better instead of blocking pain receptors."

"I heard him. I was there."

"Good. Maybe try doing what someone tells you, for once. Sometimes we have your best interests at heart."

I scratched at some filth on my clothes. "Sam?"

"Yes?"

"If I'd wanted her to abort and she refused, I'd have still had to pay child support forever. And I'd have looked like a dick. Why does she get the final word when I *don't* want her to abort? Why is she the only one who gets to decide?"

"One of the great mysteries of the world, kid. Your right of choice ended when you *chose* to not use protection."

"I know. Just doesn't seem fair." I fought down another wave of nausea and pressed the heels of my hands into my eyes. "See ya, Sam. Glad you could stop by. Let's do it again sometime."

"Do you want me to call Melissa and let her know I'll be hanging out here with you for a while?"

"God no. I just want quiet. I'll take a pill and try to sleep."

"I'll check in on you soon. Take it easy, okay? And, Xander?"

"Mmm?"

"No more booze."

"Never again. That's for sure."

"Oh, I believe that. For sure. See you later." Sam shut the door behind him with a *click*.

I twisted open the bottle of water, using it to chase a pill. I sat in silence, lost in my own dark thoughts, as the room became steadily darker.

CHAPTER THREE

Four days had gone by without a word from Lily. At least, I thought it had been four days; I could have miscounted. The warm rays of cheerful sunlight streaming through the windows were my only clue. I'd waited, unmoving, for the darkness to consume the cruel intensity of day. Life was like that. We all reached for our dreams, soared as high as we could, only to be forced to give in to the emptiness that followed. Night always extinguished the day.

Looked like the booze made me retrospective.

My phone battery had long since given out, and I hadn't gone to the effort of finding my charger. I knew I had an extra in my gym, but I really didn't want to go in there. I wasn't ready.

What if she'd tried to call me? She had the house line, but maybe she would have only tried the cell.

Shit. Why didn't I think of that before?

I should charge my phone. As well as the one in the gym, I had a charger in my bedroom. I gingerly hauled myself to my feet and approached the stairs.

I didn't like the look of those, either. With a sigh, I threw open the doors to my gym.

It was the scent that hit me first. The familiar, comforting aroma of foam rubber and plywood. The leather smell of the pommel horse. The lingering odor of sweat, tempered with broken dreams.

It staggered me.

Forcing my feet forward, I turned on the light, illuminating all the various equipment. I gazed around the room with fresh eyes. The eyes of a man returning to a home he'd once loved, but knew he would never belong there again.

I needed another drink. Snatching the charger out of the plug near my treadmill, I left the room as quickly as my back allowed and shut the doors behind me.

A search of my cabinets proved that I had finally run out of booze. Empty bottles had been scattered all over my kitchen. I picked up each, one by one, searching for anything I may have missed. Nothing.

How could this have happened? I hit the button on the side of my phone and waited with anxious, bloodshot eyes for it to power on. Dozens of notifications filled the screen, but no texts from Lily.

There were also no messages on my voicemail.

Why not? Maybe I'd missed her call but she hadn't left a message. That had to be it. I swallowed my pride and decided to call Lily. Was it pathetic? Yep. Did I care? Not really. My hand shook as the phone rang.

"Hello?" The woman's voice on the other end was unfamiliar.

"Uh, yes. May I please speak to Lily?"

"I'm sorry. You have a wrong number," she answered cheerfully.

"Oh, I'm sorry to bother you. Have a good day." I disconnected the call and frowned at my phone. How could it be a wrong number? I didn't dial a number, I just hit "Lily" on my cell phone. She had to be covering for her. I hit dial again.

"Still the same number, I'm afraid," the woman answered with a chuckle.

"But it just worked a couple days ago. Quit stalling and put Lily on the phone."

"She must have changed it. I just got this phone number a few hours ago, sir. I'm sorry."

I disconnected the call again and flung my phone onto the kitchen counter. She'd changed her number. She really was cutting me off.

Screw that. I was Xander fucking Phoenix. I could find her. I *would* find her. There was no way she could hide from me.

I shook my head. I sounded like a crazy person, even to myself. I needed to move on, needed to get *her* out of my system. Needed to *forget*. Later, though. Right now, I needed to go to the store to restock.

An angry growl reminded me that my stomach was empty, so I rifled through my fridge to scrounge some food. I grabbed the first thing I saw—a hunk of cheddar—and wolfed it down. Lifting my hands to my face, however, made me realize that they smelled awful. I lifted my arm and sniffed, wrinkling my nose. When the hell was the last time I'd showered? Had to have been before my ill-fated competition. I even still had on the same clothing I'd worn when I'd been discharged from the hospital.

I left the kitchen to eyeball the stairs. *Shit.* All my clothes were up there. This would be fun.

After Lily had told me she was pregnant, I'd kissed her and told her everything would work out. Then I left… for two days. I walked to my buddy John's place and asked to crash on his couch. It was the night before a huge qualifier. I'd wanted to drink away my troubles, but I hadn't dared with an important competition the next day. During rings, which was my signature event, I had lost focus at the worst possible moment. I'd fallen hard on my tailbone. I'd ended up with two compression fractures in my back and a dislocated shoulder. Walking would be painful for a while–maybe forever. I supposed I deserved her leaving me; I wasn't very proud of my actions. I never should have left her alone. Maybe if I'd stayed and talked it out none of this would have happened.

Slowly and carefully I ascended the stairs. I would need to move into the guest bedroom on the first floor, assuming all of Lily's things actually were out of there. I hadn't checked. If they weren't, I'd just continue to stay on my couch. Only problem was, I wasn't sure how to go about getting all my shit down there. I'd told Sam I would pitch everything over the railing, and maybe that would really work. Lifting them up that high didn't sound fun, either. Maybe I shouldn't have been so quick to dismiss Sam's offer. Whatever. I'd worry about it another time.

I wandered into the bathroom and stared at my reflection in the mirror. The man that looked back at me didn't look familiar. His short brown hair was greasy and unkempt. Four days' worth of beard marred his tanned complexion. His eyes were bloodshot, tired, and he looked like he'd aged a decade. Whoever *this* man was, he wasn't me.

I showered, then dressed quickly in sweats and a tank. Screw shaving. I didn't really give a shit, anyway. Eyeballing my closet, I decided to put off moving my stuff down. *Booze first, everything else later.*

The sun's final beams dropped out of sight as I made my way outside. The sky glowed vibrant shades of purple, red, and gold.

Climbing in my car, I took a moment to allow my back to settle. The brace I had put on pinched, and, besides, I wasn't feeling well. I had barely eaten anything for four days, subsisting instead on various bottles of hooch. At least the liquor store wasn't far. Less than five miles. I hit the red ignition button and the car roared to life.

Circling around the driveway, I decided to find a satellite station. One with gut-wrenching mood music. Or, perhaps, something angrier. Death Metal? I scrolled through one by one.

Bang! Crack!

"The hell was that?" Though no one was around to hear me, I asked out loud just the same.

Oh shit … the mailbox. I threw open the car door and tried to jump out, only to be impeded by the searing agony. I circled around the car and surveyed the damage.

Shit! Shit! Shit! Shit! The mailbox had fallen forward. The front end of my beautiful electric blue Mustang Shelby GT350R had a hideous dent.

God fucking damn it! How could I be so stupid?

I knew the answer to that. I was out of control. Fucking Lily had taken that from me, too. What the hell had I been thinking, getting behind the wheel of my car after having been drunk for days? I knew I wasn't completely sober, even now.

I was lucky it was just the mailbox.

I was *really* lucky Sam wasn't here to see this. He'd never let me live it down.

Climbing back behind the wheel of the car, I reversed and carefully backed away from the mailbox and street. Killing the engine, I googled the phone number for a local body shop.

It was time to get my shit together.

CHAPTER FOUR

Over five hundred horses rumbled over the night air as I revved the engine. The body shop had outdone themselves, finishing in only four days after quoting a week.

I had spent the time cleaning the house and moving my stuff downstairs. Everything took longer because of my injury, but I was determined to remain self-sufficient. Now that I had my car back, it was time to get out of my self-imposed exile and rejoin the world.

I hadn't been to this club in over a month. Not since... No. I wasn't going to think about her. I was here to forget. I climbed out of the car and tossed the keys to the valet, slipping the bouncer a fifty as I passed. A familiar action, even if it had been longer than normal since my last appearance. I needed familiar right now.

I skirted around the edge of the dance floor and made my way to the bar. Chrissy tended bar, her short spiky hair as pink as ever. Looked like she had gotten a few new piercings since the last time I had seen her.

I climbed carefully onto a barstool and leaned forward to catch her eye.

"Where have you been?" she asked in surprise.

"Long story. Jameson, neat. Double."

"Some things never change."

"Some things never do," I answered softly. I wasn't even sure if she could hear me over the blare of the music.

Chrissy poured the drink and regarded me in silence for a moment. "Last time I saw you, you were all over that girl and warning me off some guy that was spiking drinks. Haven't seen him since the last time I saw you." Her tone was guarded, reproachful.

"Forget about him. Forget about her. I'm certainly trying to." I lifted my drink to my lips, letting the cool liquid slide across my tongue. I winced and spit the whiskey back into the glass.

"Something wrong with it?"

I shook my head, gazing at the tumbler. "No. I just changed my mind. Make it a tonic and lime." I'd ordered the Jameson out of habit, but it was a stupid move. I'd been sober for a few days now, and should probably keep it that way.

What was I doing here, anyway? I didn't feel up to dancing; my back throbbed with every move. I didn't much want to drink, either. Doubt consumed me. Coming here had been a mistake.

I sat back on my stool and regarded the crowd. To be honest, I was here because this was where it all started. I allowed the memories to surface, embracing them.

"Hey, baby, I'm back. Did you miss me? Who's your new friend?"

God, she'd looked so beautiful even under the multi-colored club lighting. Some creep had been hounding her, sitting too close. Getting him away from her had been all too easy.

"I know his type."

"What type is that?"

"The boring nine-to-five type. They think the way to get to a woman is through their bank account. They may be stable, but rarely have the kind of money needed to really impress anyone. Simple, uninteresting, predictable. I'm sure he seemed like a nice guy, but he probably doesn't know how to please a woman in bed."

There it was. Her eyes darkened, and she licked her lips again. "And I suppose you do, then?"

"What do you think?"

"I think you're overly cocky if you think I'm nothing but a cheap blonde bimbo who will just fall into bed with you at the snap of your fingers."

She'd had spirit. Too bad I hadn't recognized her for the soul-sucking bitch she was. I could have saved myself a lot of heartache.

This was torture. I shouldn't have come here. I should have gone *anywhere* else. Orlando wasn't exactly short on night clubs.

On the edge of my vision I caught the woman next to me eye-fucking me. Pretty enough, I supposed. Curly brown hair and too much makeup. I tried to muster up my patented-Xander-Phoenix confidence.

"Come here often?" I asked, failing to meet her gaze. *What the hell was that? All the choices I could have gone with and I go with the lamest pickup line ever.*

"No. First time."

"And you're here all alone? I find that hard to believe, a beautiful woman like you."

She hesitated. "I came here with a friend, but she left with some guy, so now I'm drinking alone." She laughed, a warm and throaty laugh. My eyes darted to hers. They were a deep shade of blue, and for a moment I found myself transfixed. "You?"

"I used to."

"You look familiar." Her warm southern accent made me think of the beaches in South Carolina.

"Just one of those faces." I repeated the words I'd said so often to women, said to Lily only six weeks ago, and felt a now-familiar twinge of regret. Stifling it, I gave her a charming smile.

CHAPTER FOUR

The name Xander Phoenix had once been a household name… and by "once" I meant just the other day. They'd all forget me soon enough if I didn't recover from my back injury. The odds weren't in my favor, and I knew it. I had been with countless women, never more than once, and I didn't like to play on my celebrity to win them. I preferred a good challenge.

She had been the one exception. The only one I had ever considered a future with. I may have been sort of pushed into it, but I had embraced my decision. *Focus, Xander. Stop acting like a pussy.*

"Maybe," she said. "But I'm not so sure. You really do look familiar. I'm sure we've met before."

My smile became a little forced. "Can I get you a refill on your drink?"

"Oh, I really shouldn't. I'm such a lightweight. Put a little alcohol in me and I lose all my inhibitions." She fluttered her eyelashes.

She was too easy, but maybe I needed easy. Did I really have the energy for a challenge right now? I gestured to Chrissy, who mixed another of whatever it was my new friend had been drinking.

She turned toward me, adjusting her shirt and "accidentally" exposing her cleavage. She tossed her curly hair over her shoulder, then picked up her glass and slowly licked at the sugar rimming her glass. Taking a long pull of bright blue liquid, she tipped her head back to expose her throat.

"Mmm…" She licked her lips. "Delicious."

What was the matter with her? I tried to mask my contempt. I could be anyone. She didn't even know my name. For all she knew, I was some creep who would rape her or God only knew what.

On second thought, what did I care? I came here for a distraction, and here was one offering herself to me on a silver platter. Only problem was, despite her little show, I wasn't really interested.

No. This wasn't going to work.

"It's really warm in here. I think I'm going to step outside for some air. Enjoy your drink. It was a pleasure meeting you." I placed some cash on the bar. With a final nod, I rose to my feet and headed for the rear exit. It would be quieter this way. This whole evening had been a mistake, and I should have just stayed home.

I reached the door and kept going, making a left to circle around the building. I stared down the alleyway, pain filling my soul as well as my body. Just an alleyway. An alleyway where I had fucked Lily.

"Well, you got me out here, sugar. Now what do you plan to do with me?"

I gasped and whirled around, my back protesting at the sudden movement. It was her. My mind quickly catalogued everything we had said, trying to figure out what had led her to believe I wanted to be followed. There had been nothing. We had spoken for maybe a few minutes, at most. "I... I... but–"

"Shh... I knew from the minute you sat down next to me that you were the one I wanted to be with tonight." She closed the distance between us, a graceful tigress in stiletto heels.

I resisted the urge to back up. This was something like out of a bad horror movie. Or a porno. Or a porno-horror movie. I half expected her to grow fangs and bite me at any moment. "Is that so?"

"Yes. I always get what I want." She placed her hands on my chest, kneading my skin. "You want me, too. That's why you talked to me, why you bought me that drink. I saw you checking me out."

There were so many things wrong with this scene I didn't even know where to begin. This wasn't the way it worked with me and women. I liked the chase, the challenge. This woman was pretty enough, but not at all my type. It turned me off.

Still... I *had* come here with the intent of hooking up with someone. Maybe this could work. I just needed to take her on my terms. "I'd hate to disappoint, then. Come." I grabbed her wrist and led her down the alley to the other side of some piled up crates. I shoved her into the wall, wondering what my end game was. I couldn't pick her up. I was pretty sure she weighed more than the twenty-five pounds I was allowed to lift. Maybe I'd just get her to suck my dick. Forcing her chin up, I kissed her, pressing my tongue into her mouth. She opened to me without argument, a moan my reward.

I released her chin and dropped my hand down to her breast, roughly massaging, squeezing her hard nipple between my thumb and index finger.

Her hand came up and squeezed my hardening cock through my pants. I inhaled sharply, thrusting my hips toward her hand.

"You like that, don't you?" She grinned as she continued to rub my dick. "Touch me, sugar. Feel how wet you make me. I can't wait to have this inside me."

"You'd like that, would you? I'll touch you when I'm good and ready," I said through gritted teeth, pressing my body flush against hers, making her feel me.

"Oh, you're a tease. I'm not sure I like that, sir."

"You'll like it fine when you're screaming my name."

"Well, that would be a challenge since I don't know it."

"Xander."

"Xander," she purred. "I like that. You'll be screaming the name Rose."

Rose.

An image of a bouquet of roses and lilies lying scattered on the floor flooded my vision. *No! Lily!* A frisson of alarm jolted down my spine, and I hesitated. *Stay in the moment.* I was floored. I hadn't really been into this before, but my body had cooperated just from the stimulation. Now, though, all of that was undone as I fought off the impending panic attack.

To cover my reaction, I let my hand trail down her belly and under her skirt, seeking her warmth. My fingers skimmed up her thighs and reached the apex. I slipped past her panties…

A thong.

"Lily," I rasped, "I want to remove these with my teeth later."

"No," I moaned and backed away. It was too much. This alley, her name, her thong, my memories, my pain. All of it. I couldn't take it. I stared at her, feeling wild and out of control, breathing hard.

"Xander? What's wrong, sugar?"

"I can't do this. I can't…"

My voice broke off on a sob, and I turned from her. I wanted to run, but I hurt everywhere. All I could do was force my feet forward and pray she'd let me go. I could hear her call after me, but I couldn't deal with her. Not now, not ever. I shouldn't have come to this club. Not tonight. Maybe never again.

The hell with this shit. I didn't need a distraction, I needed Lily. I loved her. In my entire adult life, I'd never loved any woman... but I loved her. Even now, even after what she'd done. If she'd come back, I'd forgive her. I considered looking for her, but I had no idea where she was staying, where she worked, if she worked, who she was with...

"Fuck!" I shouted, not caring who heard me. I stepped up on a curb and carefully lowered myself to the ground in front of a tree, resting my forehead on the trunk.

My phone buzzed, but I ignored it.

I'd lost everything, my career, my girlfriend, my future child, and now I was losing control of my mind and body. What was left for me? Was the effort even worth it?

My phone buzzed again. I powered the device off without checking to see who'd tried to reach me.

I just wanted to go to sleep and never wake up.

I sat there in the dark. The boughs of the tree hovered over me like a bird of prey. Rose never looked for me, which was a good thing.

CHAPTER FOUR

I couldn't face her.
I couldn't face anyone.

CHAPTER FIVE

"You in for cards tonight, X?"

It had been four long months. Four agonizing months spent trying to forget everything. My back had healed as well as could be expected. I had started physical therapy four weeks ago. Things looked promising, but I still doubted my back would ever be strong enough to compete again. Even if it was, the months of not working out had set me too far back. Even now, while enduring physical therapy, it wasn't the kind of exercise that would get me back in competitive shape. Still, if it was possible, I'd find a way. I thrived on challenge.

I smirked at the phone as I pictured my buddy, John Cooke. "So anxious to part with your cash again already?"

"Gotta win it back sometime. Look, I just need to know. Sam said he could make it, but we just have the three of us. If you aren't coming, I'm cancelling."

"No pressure, though."

"Hey, man, whatever. You in or not?"

"I'll be there at eight. See you then." I hung up and glanced at the time. Only four o'clock. I pondered my options.

John had his own business; a game store and club of sorts. People hung out at all hours of the day to play various card games, roleplaying games, and weird miniature battle games. It had been a while since I'd gone to see him there during business hours, mostly because lately he had been convinced I should meet this girl who had been hanging around. Also, other than the occasional game of poker, the "gamer" lifestyle didn't appeal to me at all. Those people were weird.

I now tried to avoid women. My evening with Rose had been a low point in my life. Thankfully, I'd never seen her again, but I'd also avoided that club ever since. I'd idly flirted with a few girls since her, but any time they showed any real interest, that familiar sensation of panic welled up and I'd quickly found an excuse to step away.

I'd accepted that Lily had ruined me. Shit, she had done a number on me, and I couldn't seem to find a way to completely recover. I'd spent a few weeks desperately wishing she would come back, but eventually realized I'd never see her again. Perhaps it was for the best. Sometimes, late at night, I still thought of her and our child and what could have been, but for the most part I had come to my senses.

Four o'clock on a Friday. Surely it would be safe to go hang out at John's store for a while. I doubted it would be that crowded. Maybe being around a small group would do me some good. I grabbed my keys and headed out.

Twenty minutes later, I pulled up in front of *The Adventurer's League*. What a cheesy name. Fitting for all the weird gamers who seemed to think playing make-believe was a perfectly reasonable and adult way to spend an afternoon.

The doorbell chimed my arrival. I scanned the crowd, catching sight of John almost immediately. Only ten years my elder, his long silver ponytail made him seem older still.

"Phoenix! I thought you were coming to my place after closing." He waved, a goofy grin on his face.

I shrugged. "I had some extra time. Thought I'd come see how things were going for you."

"Things are great. I'll come chat in a bit. It's almost my turn." He gestured to the brightly colored board game in front of him.

I nodded, then went to check out some books displayed on shelving that completely lined the far wall. The scantily clad elf maidens on the covers were a sure sign that gamers needed to get laid more often. The thought came unbidden, and I tried not to dwell on how I was in the longest dry spell of my adult life. I picked up a sourcebook about elves and flipped through the pages.

That's when I heard it: a familiar laugh that sent a shock through my entire body. I turned around, looking for the source. I looked frantically around the room, checking out everyone, seeing no one familiar. I forced myself to relax and flipped another page in the book, reading about various magic items. None of it made any sense to me.

I'd been so sure I had heard her. I closed my eyes, blocking out the ridiculous chapter about magic rings. The young reporter who had asked to interview me in my personal gym over a year ago. *Faith Richardson.* Normally, I declined such requests, but something in her big green eyes had lured me in. She had seemed so awkward, so unsure of herself, so unlike any of the other reporters I'd ever met, that I had just wanted to help her however I could. She and her photographer had come and gone. The article had been mediocre and emotion-driven, not what I'd expected to see from a professional reporter. It had been... refreshing. Nothing further had come of it; I'd only ever met her twice, once when she asked in person for the meeting after nagging several times on the phone, and once in my home when she interviewed me. Despite that, she had invaded my dreams for many nights. Erotic, unexpected dreams.

It was a crush, nothing more. Also, there was no good reason for her to be here in Nerds-R-Us.

I placed the book back on the shelf and scanned the covers for another one.

"Come on, Faith, after this game I'd like to take you out. McDonalds. Please? It'll be fun." *What did he say?* I turned around again and saw a greasy-haired guy sitting at a corner table opposite a female with beautiful long auburn hair tied back in a braid. Her back was to me. They each held a few cards that swirled with bright colors, with several more laid out on the table between them.

"I can't, Mark. I have plans, I told you. Maybe some other time." Her voice, so achingly familiar, sounded annoyed.

"You always have plans. I'm sure you can make time for me just this once," he whined.

I took a step toward them, but paused. *What are you doing? You know you need to stay away from her. This won't end well. It never does. Not anymore.*

"Maybe next time," she repeated, her voice distant.

"Faith, please. I like you. I've liked you for a long time. I think we'd have fun together."

Faith hesitated. "Aren't we having fun now?"

That's it. Against my better judgment, I crossed the room and joined them, yanking out the chair next to Faith and sitting down. They both turned to look at me.

I smiled. "Hey, Faith. Long time no see."

She blinked, nonplussed. Her brow furrowed. "Mr. Phoenix?"

I chuckled. "Call me Xander. It's good to see you."

"Excuse me, Mr. Griffin, but–"

"That's Phoenix, and no one was talking to you." I scowled at Mark, angry he could be so dense. "Here's the thing, Mark, is it? I believe that Faith said no. You can just go away and leave her alone."

I looked to Faith to see how she took my speech. I knew I was coming off as heavy-handed, but something about this guy rubbed me the wrong way.

She still stared at me in complete and utter shock, speechless.

"I don't know who you think you are," Mark said, "but–"

"Name's Xander Phoenix. Google it. After you fuck off." I turned away from him, my eyes only on Faith. "The guys and I are playing poker tonight. Would be cool if you wanted to hang with us. We need a fourth. Up to you, of course."

Mark rose to his feet and stepped close, far too close. I could smell his horrible breath, which reeked of warm Dr Pepper and chips.

Without sparing him a glance, I spoke to him, my voice harsh. "You'll want to back off, unless you'd like to go outside. John wouldn't appreciate me busting up his tables for your sorry ass."

I knew he'd go. He was a typical nerdy game-playing type. Roleplaying games had taught him enough to act tough for about a second, but there was no bite to back up the bark.

Faith cleared her throat. "Poker sounds fun, but I don't know much about it. Can you teach me?"

Mark hesitated a moment more, then took off for the door, taking his cards with him. I didn't watch him leave.

"That was horrible," Faith said after the door closed. "I can handle Mark."

"I could see that, but why should you have to when I was right here? I did a much more effective job of making your point, *and,* as a bonus, got to talk to you again."

Her eyes lit up as a smile brightened her face. "It *is* good to see you again. Been a long time. How are you?"

"I'm all right. I mean, the back injury is a bummer, but it's healing."

"I'd heard something about that. So you won't be able to compete anymore?"

"Never say never, but not soon." I glanced up as John gestured to me. "Hey, looks like John finished his turn. I'll be right back, then we can talk about tonight."

She nodded and flipped through her deck of cards, organizing them. I marched over to John and pulled up a chair. "Your timing is awful."

"Is it now? I see you met Faith," John whispered.

"We've met before."

"Oh yeah? Isn't that interesting?"

"She interviewed me."

John raised his voice. "You done?" he asked the guy sitting to my right. "Pass me the dice, Phoenix. My turn again."

He rolled the dice, passed out cards, and made trades with other players before laying pieces on the board. Once finished, he passed the dice and turned back to me.

"What is this game?" I asked.

"Settlers of Catan. You should give it a shot sometime. And what do you mean she interviewed you? How?"

"She asked questions. I answered. How else do you think an interview works?"

"She works for some pharmacy, man, not a newspaper. Why would she have been interviewing you?"

"What?" I frowned, trying to assimilate that news. No. I had seen the article myself. It existed. She wrote it. Her photographer took pictures. Yes, it had been a year, but what had inspired such a drastic career change?

"You sure it's the same girl?"

"Yes," I answered, distracted. Faith had pulled out her phone and was texting someone.

"Man, I've been trying to get you to come down here for weeks. Weeks! To meet that girl… and you already had. Isn't that funny? Xander?"

I stood, ignoring him.

"Xander?"

I returned to Faith, watching the silly grin play on her lips as she tapped her screen, her cards forgotten. I wondered who she was talking to. I sat across from her, watching her silently.

"It really is good to see you again. I hadn't expected to run into you here," she said without looking up.

"Feeling's mutual."

"Well… thanks for helping me with Mark earlier…" She trailed off as if there were more she wanted to say.

"My pleasure. So…" I cleared my throat, feeling awkward, "ready for a poker lesson?"

"You really are playing cards tonight?"

"Yes, poker at John's place."

Faith glanced in his direction. She took a deep breath, her expression unreadable. "Um… are you sure you want me to come?"

"What?"

"Well, if you only invited me to make a point with Mark, I understand. I won't invade your game unless you really want me there."

"Faith, if you'd like to come, I'd love to bring you."

Her face fell, confusing me further.

"Um, well, I'd like to play cards, only I have my own car. I think I'd prefer to follow you there." She twisted her red hair, winding it around her finger and pulling the strand over her face. Obviously a nervous habit, it was both endearing and adorable.

"Sounds great. You can follow me, but I'll give you the address and my cell number just in case."

"Awesome. Can't wait. There's just one other problem, then."

"What's that?"

She giggled. "I don't know how to play poker."

I stared at the cards in her hands, though I knew they weren't standard playing cards. "What were you just doing?"

"These? These are Magic cards. My white and black angel deck." Her voice held a note of understated pride. "Not the same at all."

"Wait here. I'll teach you. Let me just go grab a deck from John."

CHAPTER SIX

I pulled into the parking lot of a twenty-four hour Mexican restaurant at eleven o'clock that night. Faith followed close behind. I was in a happier mood than I'd been in for months. She hopped out of her car and stepped onto the curb, watching me expectantly. With a grin, I climbed out and followed her. We ordered, collected our food, and found a table in a quiet corner.

"Thank you for everything, Xander. I had a blast."

"I'm glad you could join us." I wasn't so sure John or Sam were as glad , but they were too polite to say anything. Although Faith was a quick learner, her inexperience and cheerful demeanor had sent our poker game into chaos. For my part, I'd been content to sit back and enjoy her company. On our way out, she'd mentioned feeling hungry. I'd jumped at the chance to spend more time with her.

"Me, too. What were the chances of us running into each other again?" She took a bite of her plain cheese quesadilla, chewing thoughtfully.

"Slim if you're hanging out at John's store," I said with a laugh. "I don't go there often." I held out a bite of enchilada. "This is excellent. Would you like a bite?"

"No, I'm not a big fan of spicy food. Ketchup is about as spicy as it gets for me. Thank you, though. This is great. Why don't you hang out at John's?"

"Not a gamer."

"Just poker?"

"Even that's infrequent. I never had time before. But now…"

"What happened to you? I'd read you were hurt, but never heard actual details."

"Fell off the rings during a qualifier. Injured my back. Compression fractures. I'm in physical therapy."

"Does it still hurt?"

"Yes," I whispered. "But not all the time anymore. I try not to think about it."

"I'm so sorry."

"Don't be." I shook my head, my mind racing, desperate to change the subject. "I thought you were a reporter?"

"I worked on the school paper at the university."

"UCF?"

"Yes. But journalism wasn't my major. A few months on the paper and I realized it wasn't for me. Actually, I decided none of it was for me. I dropped out."

That explained why the article had been so different, so emotion-based. "What? What was your major?"

"Liberal arts. Vocal Performance, specifically."

"So you were into public speaking?" How old was this girl? I had assumed she was in her mid-twenties like me. How did I fail to notice that the article she had sent me was from a student paper?

"I was—am—a singer. I just decided I didn't need a degree for that. And it sucks, you know? Working toward a degree where your ability to pass depends on someone else's *opinion* rather than on actual skill or talent."

"A singer, huh?" I suddenly had a wicked thought. "Prove it."

"Here? Now?" Her cheeks turned an adorable shade of pink as she looked around the room. "There are people here!"

"And there are no people at concerts?"

She glared. I'd opened my mouth to ask another question and keep things moving when she surprised me.

"A love like this is like water in the desert.

I'll never have my fill, I'm burning hot like a flame.

Baby I'll drink you in. They call me a pervert.

Maybe I am, but will you think me the same?"

The restaurant went silent. Her voice was crystal clear and warm. Her speaking voice was nice, but she sounded like an angel when she sang. She blushed scarlet and sank down in her chair. "Sorry."

"That was amazing. Why are you sorry?"

"I'm so embarrassed."

I reached over and rested my hand on hers. "You have nothing to be embarrassed about. You have a beautiful voice. Are you going to become a professional singer?"

"Time will tell." She was obviously still uncomfortable. *Maybe because of the lyrics?* I considered this. I should have been having a panic attack right then, but I wasn't. Being here with her felt... right.

"John told me you work for a pharmacy. Why? That has nothing to do with singing *or* interviews." This girl was so complicated, I found myself intrigued to know more.

She shrugged. "It's good money and something to do right now. I'm a lead pharmacy technician."

"How old are you, Faith?"

"That's a rude question to ask a girl. Why not just ask me how much I weigh next?" She paused. "Twenty-one. As of last month."

"Twenty-one!" I closed my eyes. Just barely old enough to drink. Suddenly I felt very old.

"Why do you say it like that? How old are you?"

"Twenty-seven."

"That's only six years. That's nothing. My boyfriend's thirty-one. Ten years older than me."

"How long have you been seeing him?" I was careful not to show it, but that sentence had cut me. I'd felt more alive in these last few hours than I had since... since... *Don't go there, Xander.*

"Almost a year. He's another gamer." *Of course he is.* "You okay?"

"Yes, why?"

"You look like you swallowed something horrible. Your food okay?"

"My food is fine, Faith. I'm just not that hungry, after all. So are you doing any sort of concerts right now?"

"Well... I'm in a dinner theater company. We're doing *Sweeney Todd* in a few weeks." She hesitated, twisting her hair around her finger. "Will you come watch? I'll understand if you think it's silly or you don't have time."

"I'd love to."

Her face lit up. "I'll get you a ticket."

"I can't just buy one?"

"Well, you could, but I'd rather get you one. More fun that way."

"All right. I won't argue with the next American Idol."

"Shut up. That would be awesome! I was thinking about auditioning for next season if they have one. But enough about me. Tell me something about you that no one else knows." Her question and her innocent expression charmed me.

"My life is pretty much always on display. There's very little no one knows. You tell *me* something no one else knows."

"Hmm… I'm not sure."

I laughed. "Yet you expected me to have something." *Well… technically, I do have something. No. I don't talk about that. I don't even think about that.*

"Everyone always sees me as confident. The singer, the reporter, the lead tech. Always in control, always knowing what to do." She dropped her voice. "I have no idea what I'm doing and am probably the least confident person you'll ever meet."

"It's so funny you mention that."

"Why?"

"I don't often give interviews. I'd never allowed one in my own home before."

"Why did you let me?"

"Because you were different. Most reporters are confident and polished. Everything about them is fake. You seemed a little lost. Lost… but genuine. That kept me off-balance. I found that intriguing."

"Guess I can't fool you, then. Here I thought I was so smooth."

"Guess not."

"Your turn."

I sighed. I didn't like the direction the conversation had turned. I stared into her sparkling green eyes. What could it hurt? "Off the record?"

"I'm not a reporter anymore. Never was, really."

"Can I trust you to keep this between us?"

She leaned forward like a conspirator. "Did you kill someone?"

"What? You're crazy. No. Nothing like that. Well, not really."

"Tell me."

"I built my entire career around being anti-drug. Clean competition and all that. But… it's more personal than that for me."

"Oh?"

"I never talk about this."

Faith chewed her lip, lost in thought. "You don't have to if it makes you uncomfortable."

"Oh, it makes me uncomfortable, all right. But I've already started talking, so I may as well continue. I had a sister."

"Had?"

I nodded, avoiding her gaze. "Had."

"What happened?"

"She was also involved in gymnastics. It's different for girls, though. Very few are able to compete past their teens. She blossomed and had to stop. Balance had become a major issue for her. Men don't hit gymnastics prime until our mid-to-late twenties. She had to quit, and it made her horribly depressed and jealous. She'd never made the Olympic qualifiers. I did."

"I see."

"Yep. She fell in with the wrong crowd. Became addicted to booze and coke. One night... she and I got into a fight about her decisions. I could only see the risk she posed to me if anyone found out. I couldn't see the pain she was in. She got behind the wheel of her car and took off with a friend. I never saw her alive again. She got herself high and drove right off a pier. She had her seatbelt on. She couldn't remove it in time. Either that or she was too stoned to realize what was happening. Her passenger—a girl named Gloria—didn't have hers on and, ironically, that saved her life. A fisherman jumped in after them and was able to rescue her. But Gloria hit her head pretty hard, and she ended up quadriplegic. My sister died that night. Gloria died of complications six months later."

"Oh my God. That's horrible! No wonder you don't talk about it."

"My parents were devastated. We all were. We'd seen her downward spiral but were helpless to save her. She was only seventeen. Seventeen and driving high on cocaine. My parents convinced the courts to seal her criminal record, but we could do nothing to stop the press from writing about her death. At least they never found out she used. It would kill me if she were remembered that way. We were close... once. I still remember how she was before the drugs fucked her up."

"I'm so sorry, Xander." Her eyes sparkled with unshed tears. Tears for me, for my sister. I didn't want her pity. I shouldn't even have said anything. I had gone to great lengths to keep that shit covered up, and now here I was spilling my guts to someone I barely knew.

"It was a long time ago. It's okay. I just don't talk about it. A big family skeleton in my closet, that's all. So... tell me about your family."

"Not much to tell. Dad's a cop, Mom's an obstetrician. No brothers or sisters. Do you have a girlfriend?"

I hesitated. "No."

"You had to think about that, huh? I sense a story."

"You missed your calling as a reporter."

"Maybe. Maybe not. Tell me about her."

"There is no her."

She sat back and crossed her arms over her chest, prepared to wait me out.

"I've been with a lot of women, Faith. A *lot*. I was kind of known for it. They called me a philanderer, a playboy. Never seen with the same woman twice. No commitments. I liked it that way. Then one day I met a woman named Lily. Things were intense between us, even though we had little in common. She had shit taste in friends, and they all kept trying to hurt her. It was one disaster after another. I kept trying to help her, even going so far as to let her move in with me. She ended up pregnant."

"You have a kid?"

I shook my head, the familiar pain washing over me. "She left me and had an abortion."

Her hand flew up to her mouth. "Oh no. I'm so sorry. I had no idea. How long ago was that?"

"Little over four months ago."

"Still fresh, then." Her eyes were filled with compassion.

"I don't need or want your pity." My harsh words made her flinch. I felt like an ass, but she was straying into territory even my close friends avoided. I knew it was my fault for even telling her, but that didn't make her sympathy any more palatable.

"I wouldn't be human if a story like that didn't touch me."

I gave her a tight-lipped smile. "Can we change the subject, please?"

"Of course. I'm sorry. Why don't you tell me about your parents?"

After several more topics, Faith glanced down at her phone. "Oh my God, it's four in the morning! I need to get home. I have work in a few hours."

I rose to my feet and waited for her to join me. "I'm sorry to have kept you up."

"Are you?"

"Not really," I said, flashing my most charming grin. "I had fun tonight."

"Me, too. Who'd have thought I'd have been sitting here for hours just talking the night away with Xander Phoenix, the man who flies."

"Flew. Past tense. And I'm just a regular guy." *A regular guy who's had many dreams of you in dozens of positions... and now that I've found you, none of it matters. You're taken, I'm not in a good place right now. Life's funny sometimes.* "Do you believe in fate?"

"I'm not sure. Maybe in regard to some things. Do you?" We reached her car, and she leaned against the door.

"I'm starting to. Goodnight, Faith. Thanks for hanging out with us tonight."

"I had fun. Thank you for inviting me. Goodnight, Xander." She looked up at me, twisting her hair, expectation on her face. I realized I was standing far too close. Close enough that I could smell her shampoo; cherry blossoms.

Did she want me to kiss her? She sure looked like she did. My pulse sped alarmingly. Was I going to have a panic attack?

I backed away, giving her room to open the door of her older Ford Focus. I waved at her, struggling to get my pulse and erratic breathing back under control. I assumed she would be relieved I'd backed off, since I had been standing inappropriately close to a woman with a boyfriend, but she actually looked… regretful. Waving back, she climbed in her car and drove away.

CHAPTER SEVEN

I ran for the vault, leaping at the springboard and pushing it with my hands as hard as I could. Curling into a ball, I soared high into the air, spinning around three times before twisting around and sticking a blind backward landing. I raised my hands skyward and arched my back, expecting the adoration of thousands, but was instead greeted by the applause of one.

"Xander, that was incredible!" Faith's voice sounded from behind me.

I beamed. Her praise meant more to me than the accolades of thousands of nameless people. "Thanks." I turned around to see her and my breath caught.

There she stood, dressed only in a simple green nighty made of some sort of sheer fabric. I could see her nipples standing erect beneath the material. Her reddish hair was in loose waves, and her green eyes seemed to glow.

I swallowed, my mouth suddenly dry. She glided forward on long, exposed legs, her hips swaying. I wanted her. Now.

I closed the distance between us. In no time at all we were all over each other. My tongue invaded her mouth. Grabbing her thighs, I encouraged her to wrap her legs around me.

I carried her to the pommel horse and leaned her against it. Her left hand gripped a pommel while her right squeezed my shoulder. Her sharp nails dug into my flesh.

"I like green," I murmured. I reached down and followed the warmth of her body ever downward. My fingers slipped past her panties and circled her clit, then dipped inside her drenched pussy. I groaned. "Oh, Faith, you're so ready for me."

"I want you, Xander. Always. Oh God, that feels good… but I want more."

I fucked her with my fingers, curling them inside her while my thumb toyed with her clit. I stared into her eyes, completely caught in her spell. "More?"

"I need you. I want to feel you inside."

"All in good time. But… first, come for me like this."

Faith's nails dug in harder, pinching, stabbing. The pain was a welcome distraction that allowed me to hold to my resolve. Seeing her stretched across the gymnastics apparatus at my mercy, smelling her heady scent, was so arousing that it was all I could do to not take her then and there. My cock was so hard that it twitched with every beat of my heart, the skin stretched tight. I needed relief. I needed her. Soon.

"Come, Faith. I'm waiting." I slipped a third finger inside, causing her to cry out and writhe. I leaned down and drew one of her nipples into my mouth, scraping my teeth along the smooth material covering her. I sucked hard, never losing a beat with my hand.

I felt her legs stiffen. I increased my pace and pressure ever so slightly.

"Xander, fuck yes!" She screamed my name as she climaxed around my fingers. Her breathing became erratic as she moaned and squirmed.

I couldn't take it anymore. I removed my fingers and yanked her panties down unceremoniously. *"Wrap your legs around me, Faith,"* I bit out. The moment she did, I freed my dick from the confines of my sweats, lifted her where I wanted her, and plunged inside.

I set a punishing rhythm. I was so deep with her angled this way, and she cried out every time my cock reached the top of her slick channel. I bent and kissed her, demanding and taking what I wanted from her. She responded by giving me everything. Her legs squeezed me, held me where she wanted me, drove me forward. She could do nothing but hold on tight, driven as I was to lose myself in her.

She bit my lip and I groaned. I released her hips with one hand and slapped her hard on the ass before kneading and squeezing her soft skin.

"Oh shit, Faith. What you do to me," I panted.

"What do I do?"

I groaned and thrusted harder, reveling in the feel of her body gripping me, of my balls slapping against her ass. I wouldn't be able to maintain this speed for much longer, it felt too good, too perfect.

"Fuck! Spank me again!" she moaned.

I didn't need to be asked twice. I smacked her again and again, enjoying the feel of her soft skin against my hand.

Her orgasm took me by surprise. She screamed a garbled version of my name and climaxed all around me. Her pussy squeezed and milked my cock, and it was enough to send me over the edge. Stars danced in my vision as I came, and all I could hear was an intense roaring sound. I slowed down, continued to thrust into her, slowly, extending our orgasms.

The crowd continued to roar.

Oh shit.

I jerked awake with a gasp. My blood pounded in my ears, and I struggled to catch my breath. I glanced at the clock on the bedside table. It was noon. I never slept this late. I also never stayed up until five in the morning, which I guessed was a good excuse. I had missed physical therapy.

I sat up, wincing as my back spasmed. Gingerly, I stood and shoved down the boxers I had been sleeping in. Today was looking like it would be awesome. I overslept, I missed therapy, my back hurt, and I was horny as hell. Tossing the underwear in the hamper, I turned on the shower to heat up.

I stepped into the steamy water and grabbed the soap, letting my mind wander. The truth, although Faith and I had had fun talking last night, she had a boyfriend... and my gymnastics career was as good as over. Faith had been a frequent co-star in my dreams for a long time now. She'd been teasing my subconscious before I'd ever met Lily, and continued even while I was with her. She was so young, though. I'd had no idea that she was six years younger than me. And taken. I shook my head. There was a time when I wouldn't have let a boyfriend get in the way, but I didn't want to merely seduce Faith... I wanted her to need me.

The revelation surprised me. I had been celibate since Lily left me. Even my dreams had abandoned me... until now. I couldn't bring myself to trust anyone. More than that, I couldn't bring myself to care about anyone. If I looked deep inside, deep, *deep* inside, I'd be forced to admit I was afraid to let someone get close to me again.

Was it fate that I had met Faith again? If it was, fate had a twisted sense of humor reintroducing this girl into my life while she was already in a relationship. Something about her had called to me, had made me trust her last night. I'd told her about my sister, even though I had told no one since it happened. I wanted to be part of her life, wanted to know her as a friend, even if she would never let me have her.

That was it. Yes, I was attracted to her, wanted her to need me, but there was something deeper there. Though we had only just reconnected, it had felt as though we'd known each other forever. She had broken through my defenses by being a friend. With that revelation in mind, I finished up in the shower, suddenly anxious to head out to John's store and see if she was there.

I paused while toweling off. What about when we were parting? She'd looked up at me, her big green eyes pleading with me to kiss her. At least, that's what my imagination desperately tried to convince me. I had to have been mistaken, though.

Just friends.
Remember that.

"Phoenix, you came back. Twice in two days. That has to be some sort of record."

I shrugged, feigning disinterest. "I have nothing else to do these days."

"That so? Your something 'else to do' is right over there," John made air quotes with his fingers, "but I think you have competition today. I'll be done here in a bit. We'll be starting up a new Settlers game if you want to learn."

I'd known she was here. I'd seen her car before I'd even parked. I glanced where he gestured in time to catch some guy pull Faith against him and kiss her briefly on the forehead. My heart plummeted. I knew that was an unfair reaction, but it didn't make it any easier.

"No thanks, man. I'll just take a look around. I won't be staying long."

John grunted and returned to flipping through a three-ring binder filled with cards. A small crowd of kids were gathered around him, asking questions and pointing at various ones that interested them. Suddenly, I just wanted to leave, but how would that look? It was a mistake coming here.

I stared at the door, indecisive. I should go. I should leave her alone. We would never be friends, not based on the feeling of pain that hit me when I saw them together. I wanted to punch something... or someone. Someone a couple of inches taller than me and probably thirty pounds heavier, too. *The bigger they are, after all…*

I drew deep, cleansing breaths into my lungs. I couldn't think that way. I was doing too well in physical therapy to risk setting my recovery back. *Especially* for a girl I barely knew.

Then and there, in that dreadful store, I had an epiphany. I'd lost sight of who I was ever since the day I'd met Lily. *Control. Strength. Power.* I'd lost it all. My very mantra was meaningless. I needed to get my life back on track if I wanted to become the man I once was.

First thing, forget this ridiculousness. Second, I needed to call Sam. I'd paid him all these years to be my coach and personal trainer. Well, it was time that he helped me catch back up. It may be too late for this Olympic Games—I'd missed too many qualifiers—but I could train for the one after. Back injuries may be the kiss of death for most athletes, but I'd be damned if it would be the end for me.

Feeling more motivated than I had been in a long time, I headed for the door, ripping my phone from my pocket. I powered on the screen and scrolled through the contacts.

"Xander?"

Shit. I froze, grimacing. I slid my cell back into my pocket and turned slowly. "Faith."

She faltered, obviously confused at my expression. A frown creased her forehead. "You just got here. You're leaving already?"

"I told you. I don't play games."

"Except poker?"

"Rarely." I clenched my jaw as the guy who had been manhandling her approached her from behind. Okay, he hadn't really manhandled her, but he'd touched her far more than I was comfortable with. Too bad it wasn't my call. "Yes, Faith, I'm leaving. No reason to stay."

"At least come and meet Jacob?

"I–"

"Everything okay, Faith?" The tall guy's voice was smooth, confident. He wrapped his arms around her possessively. His eyes met mine, challenging me. I stared back, impassive, my expression betraying nothing.

"Yes, Jacob. Everything is fine. This is my friend, Xander Phoenix." She smiled at me. "Xander, Jacob Armistead."

On instinct, I extended my hand and gripped his, harder than necessary. "Jacob, good to meet you. Any friend of Faith's–"

"We're a little more than friends, aren't we, Faith?"

"Even better, man. Now, if you'll excuse me, I was about to head out."

Faith fiddled with a pen, tangling it in her hair, looking nervous. "Where are you going?"

"Due for a long overdue training session."

"What do you play?" Armistead asked, though his disinterest couldn't be more obvious.

I watched him a moment longer, my distrust and loathing obvious. Finally, I decided to put him out of his misery. "I don't *play* anything. I'm an Olympic gymnast. The X-Wing. Google it. See you around." I turned on my heel and left, self-righteous satisfaction making me feel invincible.

I pulled out my phone and punched a couple of buttons.

"Sam? Phoenix. Meet me at my place in an hour." Without waiting for his reply, I disconnected.

CHAPTER EIGHT

Faith had continued to visit my dreams once or twice a week, though I did my best to block her out. I was like a recovering alcoholic and had sworn off women. In fact, I had sworn off *most* distractions, save for the poker game each Friday night that I masochistically refused to give up.

She had continued to attend these games. I suspected John had had something to do with that. Fucker. He was a born meddler, worse than the little old women that considered themselves matchmakers. Regardless, I'd left alone each time, reluctant to take the risk of getting close to her, unwilling to be chased away from my friends. It had become a challenge.

I admit that part of me looked forward to seeing her each week. I had gone that first time because Sam encouraged it, but he clearly hadn't expected *her*. Nor approved. I'd been careful to avoid her gaze, even as I basked in her presence.

Speaking of Sam, I had explained to him that I was ready to get my shit together and work to take back what I once was. He hadn't seemed surprised, merely rubbed his hands together and told me to get started. My MRI had shown excellent progress with my back, so I had done two more weeks of physical therapy. Once finished, I had graduated to strenuous strength and flexibility training every single day with Sam.

Four weeks of repetitive exercises and strength-building torture later, Faith called me.

"Hello, Faith. This is a pleasant surprise. What can I do for you?" My heart raced, and I clenched my fists to tamp down the unwelcome sensation.

"I wanted to check if you still wanted to come see me in *Sweeney Todd*. I play Mrs. Lovett."

"I've never seen it, so I don't know who that is."

She chuckled. "She's an absolutely crazy woman who bakes people into pies. Come on, you'll love it. Like horror, set to music, with funny British accents."

"When?" My facial muscles betrayed me in the form of a foolish grin.

"How about this Saturday night? It's at seven."

I thought for a minute. Sam was scheduled earlier that day, so it should work out. "Okay. I'll be there."

"Great! I'll have a ticket under your name at Will Call. It's dinner theater, so come hungry."

"See you then, Faith."

"Bye. Good talking to you, Xander."

I disconnected, not trusting myself to say another word. Carefully I set my phone down, then changed clothes to stretch and start working out.

CHAPTER NINE

Flowers seemed the natural thing to bring for a dinner theater performance. Red roses, I thoought. Traditional. Timeless.

In addition to colorful bouquets, the florist stocked all sorts of knick-knacks. Delicate fairy sculptures, dragon statuettes, and hideous looking gnomes. I flipped through their collection of greeting cards, but was unable to find anything appropriate for the occasion. I decided to just get the flowers.

"Oh, my God. I know who you are!" exclaimed the blonde cashier. I smiled thinly at her, hoping she would refrain from squealing. She looked like she might be the excitable type.

"You watch gymnastics?"

"No. What are you talking about?" I stared at her, dumbfounded. How would she know who I was if she didn't follow gymnastics? She was a teenager, so I knew we'd had no history together.

"You're on the cover of *Celebrities and Sinners!* I love that magazine!"

"What?"

"Yeah, it just came out today. Haven't you seen it yet? Hang on, my copy is in the breakroom. I'll go get it."

I gaped at her as she skipped into a closed-off room. Part of me didn't want to know, wanted to leave before she came back. If she'd truly seen me on the cover of *CaS*, no good could come of it. On the other hand, I knew I needed to see how bad the damage was.

Why was it always *that shitty tabloid?*

In no time at all, she rushed back, proudly carrying her prize. She held it out to me and my heart plummeted.

Former Olympic Champion Alexander Phoenix has Sketchy Drug Past by Guest Journalist Lily A. Campbell. I snatched the tabloid from the cashier's hand.

No. I couldn't believe my own eyes. I kept reading, unable to look away, becoming more and more furious by the moment. She'd put everything out there. My sister's love affair with cocaine and underage drinking. Her car accident. Her death and the subsequent death of her passenger.

She had included quite a bit about my personal life, even going so far as to claim that I was a monster who used women as objects. The implication was that I was a hard-ass that had never gotten over the death of my sister, so I used that as an excuse to never let anyone near. My strict drug-free campaigns were called into question, suggesting that the author suspected I had an addictive personality, probably hereditary, and should be watched at all times.

This shit was slander. Or was it libel? I always mixed those two up.

There are pictures, I realized. A stock photo of me on rings graced the cover, but inside was one of me at the club, with a furious look on my face. I realized it had to have been taken the night I punched the guy who kissed Lily. Fortunately, whoever the photographer was, they hadn't captured him in the shot. The other picture showed Faith and me outside the Mexican restaurant.

The picture with Faith hit me like a punch in the gut. How had she gotten this picture? How had I not noticed it being taken? A cold chill raced up my spine.

"Will you sign it for me?" the cashier asked, oblivious to my internal war.

"I'm not the author." I pointed to the name on the front. "You'll have to ask her to sign it. She thinks she knows all about me, but all of this is complete bullshit."

"Please?"

I looked up from the magazine to see her looking at me with a hopeful expression. "Maybe if it had at least a shred of truth to it."

I tossed some bills down on the counter, grabbed the roses, and left. I called Sam from the car, hitting the button to send it through to the hands-free.

"Hello?"

"God fucking damn it, Sam. Lily wrote that fucking article, after all. It's full of sensationalized bullshit about my sister, about how I treat women like shit, and how I probably do drugs myself.

"What? Slow down. Run that by me, again."

"Did I stutter? Lily published an article in *CaS*, slamming me. I need to track down Murphy and have him force them to print a retraction."

"First of all, Murphy is out until Monday. Second of all, *CaS* is a tabloid. They aren't going to print a retraction."

"Then I'll fucking sue them. They had no right. Those records were sealed. How the hell did she sniff out the drug charges?" *Damn it!* What was the point of having a lawyer if I couldn't even get him to fix things when fucking tabloids dragged my name through the mud?

"Alexander. You need to calm dow–"

"Don't tell me to calm down! You haven't even seen that bullshit yet."

"I'm looking it up on their website now, actually."

"I'll wait."

Shit. I only had a couple of hours before I was supposed to be at the theater. This couldn't have come up at a worse time. I needed to deal with it, but I didn't want to stand Faith up.

I needed a damned clone.

"Okay, first of all, you realize the article following it is nonsense about how O.J. Simpson is really Khloe Kardashian's father, right? And further in are several articles claiming various people are cheating on other people. One so-called reporter seems to have not even gotten it through his head that 9-11 conspiracy theories were out of style last decade. This thing is uninspired nonsense. All suing them or trying to make them print a retraction will do is lend credence. Make a big deal and people will notice."

"You're suggesting I *ignore* it?" I couldn't hide the disbelief and contempt from my voice.

"Yes. Who cares what people think? Their opinions will not affect your ability to compete. The drug allegations are ridiculous, and they test you before every single competition, anyway. Negative's negative."

I realized I had pulled into the parking lot of *Celebrities and Sinners.* The parking lot was mostly empty. I stared up at the building, my lip curling in disgust.

"You know as well as I do that that's not true. Lance Armstrong was probably the most tested athlete in history, and they always came up negative. Yes, he found loopholes and ways to cheat the tests, but people won't be as trusting anymore."

"Be that as it may, you have nothing to hide. He did. This will blow over. Don't give them attention. You don't see any of the other people they wrote about demanding they remove the articles, do you? There's no point."

I looked around as though I expected to see some of these people. No one was around. "Fine. But I think this is bullshit, Sam."

I disconnected the call and got out of the car. I didn't give a shit what Sam said, I was *not* interested in becoming the next Lance Armstrong. The thought of that kind of notoriety made me feel physically sick. I'd never touched that shit. Never would.

The automatic door didn't move as I approached. The lights were off, leaving the interior dark and gloomy. No way was Lily here now.

I didn't even know if I'd be able to find her here. The article had called her a "Guest Journalist." I didn't have any idea where she could be. She didn't work here, she didn't live in the same apartment building, and she didn't have the same phone number.

Frustrated, I got back in my car and headed home to get ready for the theater.

CHAPTER TEN

The curtain opened again and all the actors and actresses filed out and bowed. I straightened my tie, which I had loosened early in the show, and brushed a few crumbs off the sleeves of my suit jacket. The crowd rose into a standing ovation, myself included, as Faith walked out on stage. Black smudges were artfully applied under her eyes, and a messy black wig concealed her long red hair. She wore a black turn-of-the-century English peasant's dress. I was astonished how incredible her voice and acting skills were. I wouldn't have recognized her if she hadn't told me who she was playing. The actor who played the titular Demon Barber of Fleet Street came out next, and the cheers of the crowd reached a fever pitch. The actors all bowed a few more times, then the curtain closed and the crowd began to dissipate.

I took my seat and regarded the bouquet of roses. I wasn't sure this was such a good idea, but it was traditional, right? Bringing flowers for an actress seemed a normal and appropriate thing to do.

I considered sending them backstage with one of the stagehands and just leaving but, truth be told, I wanted to see her. I had sworn off women, but that didn't mean I had to turn into a complete hermit. I'd seen her at last night's poker game, but we'd barely spoken a word to one another. Mostly because I didn't want to hear Sam's shit if he knew I'd planned to see her play. Now, with knowledge of that damned article hovering over my head, I wanted to do *anything* to make her not see me the way Lily had portrayed.

I waited a while longer, watching the flurry of activity as the orchestra director issued notes about the evening's performance, and various other people reset the stage back to the beginning. I was the only one left at the audience tables.

She probably didn't even know I had waited for her. I should go.

"Excuse me?" I asked a passing stagehand. "These are for Miss Faith Richardson. Can you see that she gets them?"

"Come on. I'm headed there. I'll just show you where she is."

"I'm not sure I should, I mean…"

"Look, buddy. I'm not a delivery boy. I have work to do. You want to give her those, I'll show you where the backstage dressing area is on my way past. Come or don't. I want to get home sometime tonight." He took off at a fast walk.

I followed him, feeling foolish. He banged on an unmarked door, not sparing a second glance at me before he hurried on. "In there."

One of the actresses opened the door, an unasked question in her expression. I held out the flowers. "These are for Miss Richardson."

She smiled. "Faith, you didn't tell me Jacob was coming!" she yelled into the room. "Come in, come in."

"Um… he's not. He hates musica–" I saw Faith standing in front of a mirror as I entered. She wore nothing but a black corset set and stockings. She'd taken off her wig, and makeup covered half her face. We both froze. "Xander!"

"Yes. I, um, I brought you these." I held the flowers out to her, beyond embarrassed. She ambled toward me, not bothering to cover up, and took the bouquet.

"Thank you so much. They're beautiful." She put her nose to the petals and inhaled their aroma, closing her eyes.

"You're welcome. Well… I'll just get out of your way. I can see you're busy." In fact, I was slowly becoming aware of the fact that there were many women in here, several dressed similarly to Faith. None of them seemed particularly shy, either. There was a time I would have milked this opportunity for all it was worth, but not now, not after Lily's article. Not with Faith here. Definitely not with my new goal of staying focused. Well, I'd given her the flowers. Mission accomplished. I stepped back out the door.

"Wait, Xander. Please."

I didn't turn back around. "Yes?"

"I'm starving. Debbie brought me here today, but she has to get home soon. Is there any chance I could talk you into grabbing a bite and giving me a lift home? My treat."

She wanted me to take her out? Unexpected. "Do you have anything in mind?" I tried my damnedest not to notice the bare skin peeking out between her stockings and her panties, or her ample cleavage. *Shit!* I was checking her out, and by the gleam in her eyes she had noticed.

"Anything. I'm so hungry. I've barely eaten all day." She licked her lips, and my pulse raced. "It's already after eleven, so some sort of all-night thing, I guess. Maybe Denny's?"

"Denny's… sure, if that's what you want. My treat, though."

"Thank you. I'll be out in ten minutes, okay?"

"Okay." I backed out of the room, pretending not to hear the giggling the second the door closed. "This is a bad idea," I muttered to myself, trying to block out the mental image that I was positive would be in my dreams later. "That girl has a boyfriend, and you have to focus on getting your career back, asshole."

I leaned against a wall outside the dressing room, talking to myself. I said I'd take her, so I would, but that was it. We'd go eat, I'd take her home, then off to bed for me. I had another session with Sam in the morning.

The door swung open and Faith came out, her face scrubbed, wearing black jeans and a black tank top. Her long auburn hair was messier than usual, having been freed from the braid under the wig. "Ready?"

Placing my hand on the small of her back, I escorted her to my car.

"So how was your day?" she asked.

"Actually, we need to talk about that."

"Oh?"

"My ex, Lily, published an article in today's edition of *Celebrities and Sinners*. About me, us, and my *sister*." She went silent, so I took that as a prompt to keep talking. "She accused me of being an asshole who treats women like objects, and wrote about how my sister did cocaine. She implied that I have an addictive personality and could easily go the same way Mandy did."

"Mandy was your sister?"

I nodded. I tried not to ever speak her name. It always made it more real. She'd been gone for eight years, but I still missed her, still regretted not being able to save her.

"I'm sure none of that is true." Her voice soothed me, calming my frazzled nerves.

"Some was. Most is bullshit."

"What was true?"

"Well, for starters, everything she wrote about my sister. She'd told me she found someone who knew Mandy, but also promised she'd never publish the story. Second... Faith, she's not exactly wrong about the way I've treated women. That said, I haven't been with anyone since her. Random hookups just seem meaningless now." *And freak me out like I have post-traumatic stress disorder or something. Not gonna bring* that *up, though.*

"Maybe you were just looking for the right woman."

"Maybe." My voice was hoarse, so I cleared my throat. "By the way, I enjoyed the show. Thank you for asking me to see it."

She turned her whole body toward me and grinned. "Did you?"

"Yes. You were great."

"What was your favorite part?"

"That's a tough question. I liked the whole thing, and all of you did an excellent job bringing the characters to life. I liked that they managed to take a story of a serial killer and make you feel for him. And your character, she was in love with him, but acted selfishly. You could understand where all the characters came from."

"My favorite part to sing is the one about the sea. Or the duet where they're plotting. One of those."

"Those were both great. You're very talented. Did you mean it earlier when you said Jacob wouldn't come see you?"

"Yes. He hates musicals."

"But you're in it. Why wouldn't he come to support you?"

"Just not the way he is."

"I think you told me you've been together for almost a year. Is it serious, then?"

Faith shrugged, toying with her hair and looking uncomfortable. I felt like a shit for putting that sad look on her face. We drove the rest of the way to Denny's in silence.

We settled into a curvy booth, the wall of silence still heavy between us. I couldn't take it anymore. I set the menu down. "Do you want to tell me what's wrong?"

"Nothing's wrong. Why would you think something is wrong?"

"Because you were happy, and now we're not speaking."

"Have you been avoiding me, Xander?"

I hesitated. That wasn't the response I had expected. "Have you been coming to John's to see me?"

"I asked first."

"So what?"

"Have you been avoiding me?"

"I... yes." The last word was a whisper.

"Why?"

Fortunately, the awkward moment was broken by the waitress coming over to see if we were ready. We both ordered, and the menus were whisked away.

"Why, Xander?"

I pinched the bridge of my nose and cringed. "Because you have a boyfriend, Faith."

"And that means we can't be friends?"

The air left my lungs in a rush. I didn't want to have this discussion here. I didn't want to have it at all. "I never knew they did flavored sodas here. Probably because I don't drink them. Are they good?"

A smile tugged at Faith's lips. "Yes. Sweeter than regular soda, though. You're so tense, Xander. So tightly wound." Before I knew what was happening, her hand was on the back of my neck. She rubbed and massaged the base of my neck and the back of my head. I leaned forward, placing my elbows on the table and my face in my hands. Her fingers were tantalizingly cool, and I moaned in spite of myself. I *was* tense, and her hand on me felt so good. Too good. Her touch meant too much, and I found it harder and harder to remind myself that we could never be more than friends. This wouldn't do.

"You don't have to do that," I murmured. She needed to stop. I liked it far too much. My cock had instantly hardened in response to her touch. I was so turned on, yet knew it was wrong. I considered escaping to the bathroom to splash some water on my face and get a grip, but I knew if I stood, or even leaned back, she'd see my obvious erection. I was held captive here at the table. No escape from her touch.

"I like doing it, though. You seem to be enjoying it, too."

"What?" I glanced at her, but her expression seemed innocent enough. Almost playful.

"You're moaning, silly."

"You have magic hands." Did she ever. She occasionally scratched at my scalp with her nails. It was so erotic, so sensual. I wanted her to continue forever, while needing her to stop. My cock strained against my pants, so I didn't dare move. I wished she'd massage *that*.

"Were you worried what I would think about your ex's article?" Her whispered voice so close to my ear startled me, sent goosebumps racing up my arms.

"Yes."

"She can say what she likes," she continued to whisper in my ear. "I won't believe a word of the propaganda. Exes can be vicious, and the fact that *your* ex is a tabloid reporter makes it worse."

"Thank you. That means a lot…"

The arrival of our food interrupted her erotic assault. She took her hand off me and arranged her silverware, completely oblivious to my internal struggles. My eyes darted around the restaurant, focusing on anything and everything non-sexy, trying to regain control of myself as I ate.

I cleared my throat. "So have you done any other musicals? Tell me about them…"

I walked into my home and ascended the stairs in a daze. This couldn't be happening. I had done such a great job getting my life back on track, and now, with a single flash of green eyes, it was all undone.

There was a time I'd thought I'd fallen for Lily. I truly had. I could see now that it was a farce. She and I had shared a harrowing experience that drew us together. Then, after I injured my back, she represented a shift in my priorities; a back-up plan. She had been right to leave, but I could never forgive her for the abortion *or* for the article.

Faith occupied a place in my soul that Lily had never been able to touch. It would be my luck that the first person I'd ever completely and irrevocably fallen in love with would be off limits to me. I had felt it from that first night together at the Mexican place. Perhaps it was just because I couldn't touch her, but I doubted it. My feelings for Faith *felt* deeper. They felt like more. *Love.* I had tried to deny them, tried to block them out, but they were there. And it was all for nothing. Her heart belonged to another.

I turned on the television and flicked to the music channels. Pausing at the grunge station, I cocked my head to the side and started to laugh. *"My Sacrifice"* by Creed. Wasn't this song almost fifteen years old? Why would it be playing now other than to mock me? I stood there and listened to the entire thing, rubbing at the sudden pain in my chest. Yes... my sacrifice. I would have to let her go. In the end, it would be better for us both.

Faith...

I missed her already, grieved like I'd lost her, and she'd never been mine.

Never *would* be mine.

Chapter Eleven

Faith called me the next evening just to chat. Our easy banter covered everything from her play to our favorite foods. Because of her work schedule, she apparently didn't head out to the *League* as often as I'd thought. A small, petty part of me was happy she'd called for no other reason than it meant she wasn't with Jacob, wasn't doing things with him that I wished she'd do with me. I fell asleep that night with a smile on my face.

Monday morning found me calling Murphy, my lawyer. He urged me to listen to Sam's advice and to let it go. Yes, there were grounds for a libel case, but he felt that making a big deal out of it would only serve to make *them* popular and make *me* look worse.

I didn't like that answer from Murphy any more than I'd liked it from Sam.

Arriving at the *CaS* building, I took a moment to look around the parking lot. I wasn't sure what I was looking for; Lily didn't have a car when I last saw her. Finding nothing out of the ordinary, I entered the building and called for the elevator.

Everything was eerily similar. The same stark, boring walls. The same receptionist behind the clear glass window. I tapped the glass.

"I have an appointment with Lily Campbell."

"Hmm…" She flipped through her books. "I don't see anything on the schedule for Ms. Campbell. Let me check with her. Have a seat."

"I was surprised to hear from Ms. Campbell. I thought she didn't work here anymore." I flashed my most charming smile.

"She just came back last week. Go ahead and have a seat. I'll just let her know you're here. I'm sorry, but what is your name again?"

"Alexander." She stared at me expectantly, waiting for me to continue. "That's all. She'll know who I am."

The receptionist looked like she wanted to say something more but thought better of it. I waited less than a minute before a confused looking Lily opened up the door. "I'm sorry, Mr–Xander!"

She gaped at me, looking for all the world like she'd seen a ghost. I crossed the room to her. "We need to talk."

"How did you…? When…?"

"Not here, Lily. Come outside with me."

That seemed to shake some reason back into her. "I'm not going anywhere with you."

"You'll come outside with me, or we can do this right here. Your choice." The set of her chin told me she wasn't going to budge. I held up my phone, which had been opened to the *CaS* website. "So many things I want to say about this. How *dare* you bring up my sister? Hadn't I made myself *crystal* clear that she was off limits before? How could you? And the rest of this... we both know it's bullshit. I want to know *why* you've gone on a one-woman crusade to try to ruin my career, which, by the way, won't work. Not this way."

Her voice raised, clearly so others could hear. "I don't know what you mean, Xander. Your sister's death was public record."

"Fuck that. You know what I'm talking about. Don't play stupid."

"You knew I had that info. I'd told you."

"You'd also promised not to go public with it." My eyes narrowed. "And this other stuff. Addictive personality? Treating women like objects? *Violent?*"

"I stand behind it. It's an opinion piece and *that* is my opinion."

"So my proposing to you was a side effect of my addictive personality? Fuck you, Lily. Why now? Why..." I tapped the screen and held it up to her face. It was the picture of Faith and me outside the restaurant. "Where did you get *this* picture?"

"Anonymous photographer. Are we done yet? *Some* of us have work to do."

"Not yet. Explain to me why you've done this. What is different about *now* instead of *then*?"

Her hand went to her slender belly. The gesture wasn't lost on me, though I didn't think she was aware she did it. A tiny diamond chip sparkled from a ring on her left hand.

"Needed the money. *CaS* was more than happy to pay me for the scoop."

"How much do they offer for backstabbing and betrayal these days?"

"Dramatic much, Xander?"

"I don't think so. I told you over and over that my family was off limits. You disregarded that, *and* included bullshit lies about me." I gestured to her ring. "Get a better offer?"

Her small hand curled into a fist, then she hid it from my view. "What's it to you? I've seen you with the redhead. Isn't she like thirteen? Still has her baby fat. Maybe I should write about *that* next."

"Fuck you! If you *ever* write about me ever again, or about anyone I care about, you'd better make *sure* that every single word is true, or I *will* sue the shit out of you for libel so fucking fast your head will spin. No more making shit up."

"Keisha, call security. Mr. Phoenix is done here," Lily shouted.

"No need, Keisha. I have nothing more to say to this lying, conniving bitch anyway. I meant what I said, Campbell. You'll be wise to remember it." I turned to leave.

"He's just pissed because his new girlfriend was undoubtedly shocked when she saw the article. She probably dumped his sorry ass," I heard her say as the stairway door closed behind me.

I didn't take the bait. The only thing it would have accomplished would be getting me kicked out. Sam would be pissed if he found out I'd confronted her, but I didn't give a shit.

I decided to go home and lay low. I didn't want to see anyone, didn't want to talk to anyone. I pushed myself into my workout regimen as if working hard enough would make all my troubles go away. Sam didn't question my motivation, luckily for me.

When Faith called that night, I tried to get off the phone, claiming I wanted to watch a movie. She harassed me until I named one, then complained she had never seen it before. Despite my bad mood, I found myself inviting her over to my place. I popped popcorn, and we sat on the couch to watch together. By the time she went home, I still had no idea what the movie had been about. My thoughts had been consumed by daydreams of Faith and me. It had been all I could do not to pull her to my chest and kiss her, but somehow I'd managed to behave myself.

Jacob was a lucky bastard. I wanted to beat the shit out of him out of spite.

Faith continued to call me over the next couple of evenings, but Thursday night I found myself missing her voice. She never called.

She had phoned every evening for the last four nights. Where did she go? I rifled through my old CD collection and found what I was looking for: *Best of Creed.* I popped it into the Blu-ray player and wondered if it would be able to read the ancient, scratched disc.

Finding *my* song, I sat down on the couch and brooded. When it finished, I started it again. *My Sacrifice…* yes. I had to stop thinking about her; she wasn't mine. I turned the volume down and hit repeat on the song. Lying on the couch, I let the music wash over me.

The ringing phone startled me awake. When had I fallen asleep? I grabbed the remote and shut off the still-repeating song. I glared at the phone. Two in the morning.

I grabbed it. "Faith, are you all right?"

"I'm great, Xander." She paused. "Did I wake you?"

"Yes, but it's okay. I'd wondered where you were."

"I just wanted to say goodnight before I went to bed."

I couldn't help smiling. "Did you?"

"Yes. I had the best night."

"What happened?" Silence answered me. "Faith?"

"You sure you want to know?"

No. "Of course. Tell me."

"Jacob finally told me he loves me. I'm so happy."

Words failed me. Logically, I knew I had no right to be upset. Her heart wasn't mine. Never had been, and never would be. But my heart and brain didn't feel like being logical right then, so I said nothing.

"Xander... Xander? Are you still there?"

"I... yes. I'm here."

"What's wrong?"

Is she actually this fucking dense? "Nothing, Faith. I'm so... um... happy for you. I'm happy you're happy. Yup. Happy." *Great. Now I'm rambling like an idiot. A manic idiot. My sacrifice... my sacrifice...* the words repeated in my head.

"I–" Faith sounded as much at a loss as I felt.

"I'm going to go back to sleep, Faith. I'll talk to you some other time, okay?" I hung up, but instead of going to sleep, I got up and foraged through the kitchen for a drink. "I'll see you in my dreams."

I was on my third beer when a pair of headlights lit up my entryway. Who in the hell would be here at three in the morning? When the lights were shut off, I was able to make out the shape of Faith's car. I opened the door and waited, the breeze raising goosebumps on my naked chest and arms.

She approached me slowly. "Xander?"

"Everything okay?"

"I came to check if *you* were okay. You sounded strange on the phone."

"You *are* aware what time it is, right?" The look of hurt and humiliation of her face made me relent. I'd put that look there. She'd been happy less than an hour ago. I sighed. "Come inside, Faith. You came all this way."

I held open the door and waited while she passed me. Why was she here? What did she want? Was she here to rub it in even more?

Fuck that. Maybe it was the third beer I had just finished, but I was tired of acting like a pussy where she was concerned. Here she was, three in the morning, in *my* home. She came of her own free will... to see me. This was my sign.

I shut the door behind her and set the bottle down on an end table with a *thump*. I crossed my arms over my chest. "Why are you here?"

"I was worried."

"About what?"

"You."

I continued to watch her, my gaze impassive.

"Xander, why are you looking at me that way?"

"Do I make you uncomfortable?"

She walked up to me, close enough I could smell the delicious scent of cherry blossoms. "You could never make me uncomfortable."

My growl rumbled deep in my chest. Before she could move a muscle I was on her. I grabbed her in my arms and backed her into my front door. Pressing my mouth to hers, I demanded her surrender. She felt stiff in my arms, hesitant. After a moment, though, she relaxed and opened her mouth. My tongue plunged inside, taking no prisoners.

My arm wound around the small of her back, pulling her flush against me, letting her feel my cock harden even more by the second. Her tongue stroked mine. Her mouth tasted fresh and cool, like she'd recently brushed her teeth. Everything felt so right. *This* was where she belonged.

She was *mine*. Not Jacob's. How could she be? My entire body tingled with the intensity of our connection. She had to feel it, had to feel how right we were for each other. How could she not?

Her moans vibrated through my lips, spurring me onward. This was all too much. I broke away first, gasping for breath.

"Faith…"

There she was, trapped against the door in front of me. Her lips were swollen by the passion of our kiss. She'd never looked more beautiful. Her brilliant green irises glowed, just as I'd always imagined them.

"You are so beautiful," I finished.

She smiled. "You're drunk."

"Hardly. Trust me, Faith. I know exactly what I'm saying."

Her face paled. "Then… you–"

"Shh… don't say anything, I need to get this off my chest. That night at the Mexican place. It meant so much to me. I told you things I've never talked about… and I didn't understand why. Now I do. I love you, Faith. I have for some time. You've haunted my dreams since the day you interviewed me. You told me tonight that another man had confessed his love for you. I know I didn't take it well. It's because… because… I wish it were me you wanted."

"Oh my God."

I kissed her forehead, unable and unwilling to let her go. "Choose me, Faith. I've been waiting for you for so long. Can't you feel this," I waved my hand between us, "this connection? I told myself to put you from my mind, told myself I needed to focus on gymnastics, but when it comes down to it, I can't deny how I feel now that you're here. And that kiss... you feel it, too. If you didn't, you'd be home asleep right now."

Faith stared at me, her mouth hanging open. It would have been comical if I wasn't so serious. Without warning, she launched herself at me. I twisted to catch her and suddenly we were all over each other. Her fingers tangled in my hair and scratched at my scalp while my hand plunged under her shirt to rub her breasts. She wrapped her leg around my waist and ground herself against me.

I broke away again. "Shit. Faith... are you sure?" My eyes searched hers. I could tell that she meant it, knew that she wanted me, but I worried that she may be just lost in the moment. She nodded, and my heart went into overdrive. I was desperate to hear her say the words. "Say it."

She licked her lips. "Xander, I've been denying how I feel. I've been with Jacob for so long, for all the wrong reasons. It had become a habit. I didn't want to hurt him, but I haven't been able to get you out of my mind, either." She rubbed her hand along the stubble on my cheek, and I leaned into her touch. "I was afraid to hope that you would want me. Now I'm afraid I might be dreaming. Make love to me. Make me yours."

"Mine…" I scooped her up in my arms and carried her to my bedroom, thankful that my back had healed so well. She was curvy but light in my arms. I barged through the open door and laid her on my bed, then stepped back to admire her. Much as my body urged me to claim her, to lose myself in her, I wanted to savor this.

She sat up and started to remove her shirt, but I stopped her. "Let me undress you. I want to do it."

"Did you mean it when you said you've been dreaming about me?"

I smiled as I removed her strappy sandal and lifted her foot up, kneading the arches. Ducking down, I licked her Achilles' tendon, thrilling at the sound of her sharply inhaled breath. "Yes. I've been dreaming of you for months. Ever since you interviewed me." I reached for her other shoe.

"What did you dream?"

"I'll show you tonight." A grin stretched across my face, full of promise.

Her eyebrows lifted. "You've been having *sex* dreams about me?"

I paused. "Not every time, but yes." I sucked on her other ankle, kissed her foot. "Do you still believe in fate?"

"Yes," she breathed.

"Me, too." I rose up on my knees to unbutton her jeans and pulled down the zipper.

"Wait." I froze, worried that she was having second thoughts. "You said you've been dreaming of me since the interview?"

"Yes."

"That was over a year ago."

"Believe me, I know."

"But what about your ex? She was more recent."

"Are we seriously going to do this now? I thought you wanted me to make love to you."

"Please. I need to know."

I swallowed. She may not like this answer. I shouldn't have mentioned the dreams. Now she thought I was an obsessed weirdo.

"Faith… I dreamed of you while I was with Lily. I never told her. I didn't even understand why. It wasn't every night. It wasn't even every week, but often enough… and always you. No one else."

"Did you know I would be at the *League* that day? Was everything… planned?"

"No. God, no. Listen, John *had* been trying to get me to come down and meet a girl that had been hanging around, but I had no idea he meant you. Trust me, I was beyond shocked. I'd assumed I'd never see you again. Also, to be honest, I haven't been with anyone since Lily, and I had no plans to.

I really was just there that day because I was bored. Meeting you again was completely by chance. Getting involved with Lily was the kiss of death for my gymnastics career. I may never recover, but I'm going to try."

"You'll do it," Faith whispered. She leaned forward and kissed my bare chest. "I want to kiss you here," she said, her hand traveling to my stomach. I stilled and closed my eyes. Her fingers were oh-so-close to brushing against my cock, but she stopped short. I hummed low in my throat and pushed her back onto the bed.

"My turn to explore first. No more talking. I mean it." I eased her jeans down over her hips, exposing her lacy black panties. Lifting her ass up, I pulled both off and dropped them on the floor. I kissed my way up her legs, around the backs of her knees, and bit the inside of her thighs, breathing in the scent of her needy pussy.

"Christ, Faith, you smell incredible. I can't wait to taste you."

She rose her hips toward me. "Then don't."

I dipped a finger inside, then withdrew and popped it in my mouth. I moaned my appreciation. "Mmm ... delicious."

I climbed up her body and hovered over her, tracing her full lower lip with my finger. "Taste."

Faith opened her mouth, and I nudged my finger inside. Her lips closed around me. Her tongue swirled around my finger, stroking me. My cocked throbbed in response, her talented tongue driving me wild.

"*Fuck...* what you do to me, Faith." With a mischievous gleam in her eyes, she bared her teeth, clamping down. I groaned and gently tugged my finger free.

I grasped the hem of her shirt and pulled it up and over her head, exposing her matching black lace bra.

I climbed back on top of her and kissed her, dry humping her through the barrier of fabric that still separated us. She grinned and reached between us, her hand tunneling under my waistband and gripping my shaft. "Oh shit," I whispered as she squeezed me.

"You like that?"

"I think it's obvious."

"Show me."

"Soon enough." I squirmed away, desperately trying to hold onto my self-control. I wanted nothing more than to strip myself bare and let her do as she wished to me, but first it was my turn. I kissed down her chin and neck, down to her breasts. I pulled each one free of her bra, pushing the cups down so they lifted each breast up.

"Your tits are gorgeous. You know that, right?" I massaged one, her flesh more than filling my hand, as I bent to lavish attention on the other. My tongue swirled around, much the same way she did with my finger. I flicked her nipple, then sucked hard, scraping my teeth around the edges of her areola. After a few minutes, I switched breasts, offering the same attention to the other.

Faith moaned and arched her back, trying to encourage me to suck harder. She clearly loved having her tits played with. I pinched and rolled her other nipple between my fingers, tugging on them. I'd bet Faith would love some clamps. Maybe I'd get her some later.

Faith squirmed and cried out, lost in a sea of sensation. Her hips pumped, desperate for friction. I slowly eased my hand down and palmed her, applying a small amount of pressure on her clit but not moving. Not yet.

Quickly, I switched breasts again and bit down, drawing her flesh into my mouth.

"Oh my God, Xander, I'm so close, so close… oh please. Please. Xand–" Her cry became garbled as she became lost in her climax. Shifting my hand, I rubbed her clit with my thumb, extending her orgasm and driving her wild. I couldn't keep this torture up for much longer. I needed her, needed my own relief.

"I love it when you scream my name. Do it again." Darting back between her legs, I licked her pussy lips, which were still swollen from her desire. I rubbed her clit with my thumb in small circles, matching the pace I'd set with my tongue.

"Oh please…"

"Please what? Tell me what you want."

"No… Xander, I need you."

"You'll have me soon enough. I can't wait to slide myself inside you, to feel your hot, wet cunt squeezing me, milking my dick." I closed my mouth over her clit, sucking hard. She cried out. Pressing my advantage, I thrust two fingers inside, finger fucking her. In perfect rhythm, I flicked my tongue to the side. She jerked, whimpering. I repeated the gesture again and again. Her legs tightened around my head and I knew I was on the right track.

"Ahh… that's so good. Don't stop." She bucked as my fingers found just the right spot inside. I had her right where I wanted her. I closed my lips on her skin and sucked, never missing a beat, even as she screamed again, her legs locking around my head and her back arching as she ground herself against my face. Her tight pussy became even tighter as she pulsed around my fingers. I kept up my relentless torture until her climax ended, then licked the juices from her cunt, savoring her flavor.

My cock throbbed, aching for her, pre-come already beading at the tip. I couldn't hold off any longer. I tugged open the drawer in my bedside table, thankful that I still had the box of condoms I had bought so many months back. Dropping my pants, I ripped the package open and rolled it on while she watched me. She licked her lips, her breath coming fast.

I climbed back on top of her, balancing on my forearms, lining myself up. I kissed her, pressing my tongue past her lips, loving the fact she could taste herself on my tongue. Her eyes closed, and I missed seeing her glowing emerald eyes, beautiful like a precious gemstone, gazing up at me.

"Faith… open your eyes. I want to see you. Are you ready for me?"

Her eyelids fluttered open, out of focus. "Mmm…"

I grinned. "I hope 'mmm' means you're ready, because I refuse to wait another second." In one swift move, I impaled her, my aching cock sliding deep inside. I pressed my forehead against hers, needing a moment. At this rate, I would blow my load in under a minute, and that wouldn't do. She deserved so much better. I wanted this to last. I held perfectly still, focusing on breathing and relaxing my overexcited body.

"You okay?" she whispered, squirming beneath me.

"Yes. Don't move. Shh…" I kissed her chastely on the forehead and mouth, holding still. "Feels so good. I want to savor the moment, that's all." Soon I had myself under control again, and slowly I began to move.

Her eyelids slid closed again as she offered her mouth up to me.

"Open."

I kissed her, picking up the rhythm slightly, losing myself in her. Nothing else mattered besides our little bubble. The entire world could have gone up in flames and I wouldn't have cared, so long as we were safe and together… right here, right now. "I want to hear you. Talk dirty to me. Tell me what you want."

"I love how your big cock feels inside me, filling me to the brim. I want you to fuck me… hard. Fast." Her voice, low and urgent, spurred me on. Unable to resist, I increased the pace and depth of my strokes, driving myself into her, pushing us both closer and closer to ecstasy. I angled my hips to hit a different spot inside her, making sure to grind my pelvis against hers to stimulate her sensitive clit.

"You are mine," I bit out.

"Yes. Yours."

"This pussy is mine. Mine! Say it, Faith!"

"I'm all yours. This pussy is yours."

Now I was the one to close my eyes against the onslaught of emotion welling up. "Mine... yes. Come, Faith. Come for me."

Without another word, she let go. I gritted my teeth, trying to ride out the exquisite feeling of her pussy clenching all around me. It was in vain. The delicious pressure built in my balls, and as she started to slow, I pumped hard into her twice more, my load forcing its way up my shaft and inside her. I roared, unable to stay silent.

As I held myself up with my arms, trying to catch my breath, I felt something inside my soul shift. I stared deep into Faith's eyes and realized I couldn't imagine ever being without her. The world made sense... Everything before seemed chaotic and confusing, and thinking about a future without her was inconceivable. I really did want her to be mine, and couldn't understand how I'd survived this long without her. I realized with startling clarity that I *trusted* her. I trusted her when I had been convinced I'd never trust a woman again. *That* was why I told her all that shit about my past, about Mandy. I'd trusted her even then.

I kissed her gently and rolled to the side, overcome. That was the best and most intense sex

I'd ever had. Always before, sex had been about scratching an itch, and sometimes about passion. With Faith, the passion was definitely there, but it was fueled by love, by a connection.

I glanced at the glowing digital clock on the bedside table. Nearly five in the morning already. I pulled her up to my pillows and tugged the blanket over us. "Sleep now, baby." I kissed her on the forehead. "Goodnight."

CHAPTER TWELVE

My phone rang. I tried to reach for it, but a weight held my left arm down, preventing me from moving. Distantly, I heard the chime of the doorbell downstairs. I leaned my head forward and found the top of Faith's head. Smiling, I kissed her, completely relaxed. The ringing continued.

Shit! Sam!

I squirmed free and grabbed my phone. "Phoenix."

"Where the fuck are you?"

"Good to hear from you, too, Sam."

"Don't give me that. It's ten-fifteen. I've been trying to reach you for twenty minutes. Your car is here, where are you?"

"Upstairs. Be right down." I disconnected. Leaving Faith to sleep, I grabbed a fresh pair of boxers and workout pants and hurried downstairs.

I threw open the door to see Sam's angry face, his arms crossed over his chest. "What the fuck, Xander?"

"I'm sorry. I overslept."

"Right. And why would that be, I wonder?" He pointed to Faith's car. "You told me you were going to take this seriously, that you weren't going to get caught up with women again."

"I *am* taking this seriously. Come in. Let's get started."

"Where is she?"

"Asleep. Don't worry about her."

"For how long? Until she's pregnant, too?"

I hit him before I realized what I'd done, my fist connecting with his cheek. Sam staggered backward, almost falling. He cupped his face, rubbing it, his pale eyes blazing with fury. He stepped into my space, a menacing scowl contorting his features.

"Don't, Sam."

"Or what? You'll hit me again? Fuck this, Alexander. You're a God damned mess. I didn't sign on for this. I agreed to be your coach and personal trainer, but you can't focus anymore. You weren't even this out of control as a teenager."

I took a deep, steadying breath, determined not to prove him right. "Come inside, Sam."

"I think I'll stay right here. Good chance I'll just leave. I'm sure there's some other out-of-control punk I can train into a star. Why am I wasting my time with a man who doesn't want my help?"

"Get inside, asshole. I'm sorry I hit you, already. Damn it. You *know* Lily is a sore spot. Wouldn't it be for you?"

We stood there, both stubbornly glaring at each other. Finally, Sam sighed and shook his head. "Damn it. I'm sorry, too."

I flexed my hand, drawing Sam's attention there in an instant.

"You idiot. Did you hurt your hand?"

I held it up so he could see it was uninjured. "Nope. I'm good. Let's get started."

Once through the double doors of my gym, I dropped to the floor and started stretching.

Sam followed, circling around me and watching my form.

I glanced at him. "You know you're more than just my trainer."

He grinned, then winced and rubbed his jaw. "Don't turn into a chick on me. I already have a wife."

"I should get one of those someday."

"Maybe when you grow up, son."

I chuckled. "Listen. Don't worry about Faith. I'll talk to her. Getting back on track is my first priority. I swear. I won't let a repeat of what happened with Lily become a problem again."

"Glad to hear it, hotshot. Listen, I want you to have another MRI. I've scheduled you an appointment on Monday."

"Shit, I hate those things. Why?"

"Damn it. That was a mean right hook. I keep almost smiling and my face hurts. I have news."

"I already apologized. I still think you deserved it. Hitting below the belt and all that. Why do I have to have another MRI?"

"How's your back been?"

"My back's been fine. I've been a little sore off and on, but nothing over the top. I hadn't worked out in three months when I started PT. After that, we jumped right into strength training, so I figured the soreness is normal."

"It is. I'd like you to start attending competitions and qualifiers again."

I stopped stretching and stared at Sam as though he'd just started speaking German or something. "Why?"

"Show everyone you're back in action. Show your *sponsors,* especially, that your injury was temporary and you want to fight to reclaim your place. Look, I'm gonna level with you. You're so far behind after bombing at that last qualifier. Not to mention missing the event in Calgary. You have pretty much no shot at these Olympics."

"Then why?"

"Show the world that you're a fighter, Phoenix. Show *yourself* that you can do it. All of them know what happened, now show them what you're made of. The odds of you getting enough points to make this team are virtually nonexistent, but you never know what'll happen."

"And the MRI?"

"The MRI is to ensure that you haven't done any damage since you stopped PT." Sam paused. "Look, I'm not gonna lie, when we got the results from the hospital after your injury I was sure you were done. Compression fractures almost never heal well enough to provide the kind of strength you'd need to continue… if it even heals straight at all. Against all odds, yours did. You're still young, healthy, in fighting shape. You've lost nearly five months, but if you are truly determined, I think we can get you back where you need to be to at least not embarrass yourself."

"I don't know. Simply not embarrassing myself isn't really good motivation."

"Time to fly again, Phoenix. Show them that although you've lost your shot at the next Games, you're willing to fight every step of the way and will still be fighting for the next one."

"Why would they even let me compete?"

"Are you kidding?"

"No."

"Because you're the X-Wing. Because your name is known worldwide. Because I've already made the call and you're tentatively approved for Beijing."

"What? How? I've lost my sponsorships, no doubt."

"Not at all. They've asked me for a copy of your MRI. You'll need to sign a release, and I'll send it along after you get the next one. They seem very curious about your recovery. They haven't given you the green light yet, but I'm confident I can talk them into it."

"Holy shit. When were you going to tell me any of this?"

"Today, idiot. That's why we're having this conversation. I've been making phone calls for the last week."

"All right, Sam. Where do we start?"

"Well, today we're going to put you back on an apparatus. Still deciding which one. We're gonna take it slow to see how you feel. Tomorrow we'll push harder. Sunday, harder still. We'll work you on Monday, assuming you're holding up okay, then head out to the imaging center. You have to swear to me that you're fully on board, though. I won't go to your sponsors if you're going to just fuck around and do shit by halves."

I was starting to feel a little excited by the idea, as daunting as it was. I opened my mouth to answer, but caught movement out of the corner of my eye. Faith stepped in, looking confused.

"I didn't know where you'd gone."

I pointed to the bench Sam occasionally occupied. "Faith… sorry, but it was time for training. Take a seat if you'd like."

I felt Sam's eyes boring into me, but I ignored him. Faith looked between us, seeming a little flustered. She was looking for an escape, clearly. Well, this was my life. She'd have to get used to it if she planned to stick around. Finally, she walked over to where I had indicated and sat.

I nodded to Sam. "You have my word. I don't know if I'm ready yet, but there's only one way to find out. I will do my level best, and I *will* stay focused."

"Good. Feeling limber yet? Let's see what you make of the rings."

I hopped up and grabbed my grips from the shelf. I approached the rings, eyeing them. My chosen event. I favored rings, loved the power and control needed to perform them well. *Power. Strength. Control.* I smiled as I remembered my mantra. "You sure rings is the best place to start?"

"Well, it's the one you fell off, and they say if you fall off a horse, get up and climb right back on. Also, pommel, parallel and horizontal bars, vault… you'll be moving fast. Anything can happen. Rings are slower. I want you to really feel as you go. Listen to your body. How's your hand?"

"My hand?"

"The one you fucking… I mean…" Sam glanced at Faith. "The one you hit me with."

I flexed my fingers. "It's fine. Your face is swelling, though. I have ice packs in the freezer, you know."

"I'll get it later. Let's get you up there. I want to keep an eye on your form. Ready?"

I nodded. Sam circled around behind me, placing his hands on my waist. I jumped and he lifted to help guide me into place. I took a moment to acclimate myself, adjusting my hold and position, then allowing my body to hang straight down, supported by just my arms.

"You okay, Xander?" Sam asked.

I nodded. "Feels great."

"Okay, hotshot. Start through one of your practice routines. Extend counts, cut out all fast swings, and no dismount today. If you feel any back pain, get down immediately."

I spread my arms into an Iron Cross, holding and counting. Then, slowly, I rolled backward into a handstand, careful to not jar the straps too much.

"How's that feeling?"

"I swear, Sam, sometimes you're worse than a parent. Stop distracting me. I lost count." I switched position into an L-sit.

"Just don't do anything stupid."

I continued through my routine, focusing on form and extending counts out a little bit longer than normal. I felt great as I moved into the second-to-last position.

"I've got this, Sam. I feel great. I'm sure I can manage the dismount."

"Screw that. One step at a time; I don't want you reinjuring yourself. Just drop into position one and let go."

I rolled my eyes. "You worry too much."

"You do that dismount right now, and you'll be looking for another coach... assuming you can still even walk."

I extended my arms, lowering myself down as far as possible before letting go, landing lightly on my feet. "Fine, I'm down. Happy?"

"Ecstatic. Thanks. How are you feeling?"

"Like anything is possible. My back feels fine. I can't believe it."

"How about muscle weakness? I saw a bit of trembling from the straps."

I nodded. "A fair bit. I can tell it's been a while. No pain, though."

"I think you looked great up there!" Sam and I both turned to look at Faith, who was sidling up to us.

Sam frowned but otherwise ignored her. "Anyway, the muscle weakness is a correctable issue. Repetition will sort that out. We'll need to work up to the faster elements, too. Maybe horizontal bars tomorrow, if you aren't too sore. In the meantime, bend over and place your hands on the floor. I want to check your back."

I bent over, waiting while Sam felt my spine.

"Any tenderness?"

"No. None."

Sam whistled through his teeth. "I wouldn't have believed it. You are one lucky son of a bitch, Phoenix. If you feel up to it, I'd like you to do thirty minutes on the treadmill, then fifteen minutes of free weights."

"Sam, I'm fine." I checked the time and powered on the treadmill.

"Just want you to stay that way. If you'll excuse me, I'm going to hunt down that ice pack now. Be back in a minute." I didn't respond as he left the room, leaving me alone with Faith. I ignored her, settling into a jog.

I saw her get up out of the corner of my eye, but I didn't acknowledge her in any way. A small voice inside my head worried that she would grow impatient and leave. I was afraid that she would regret last night's decision... but... if it was to happen, I'd just as soon want it to be now instead of later. I clenched my jaw, regaining my focus as I hit my stride and began to run full out.

Faith explored my home gym. She touched every apparatus, running her fingers gently over each one. Then, with a glance at me, probably to see if I'd stop her, she started checking out the framed photos on the walls. Most were of me at various competitions. There were a few of my competitors' photos as well. Several of me holding medals and ribbons, many newspaper articles. There were even a few motivational posters I'd posed for. I knew what she was doing, though. She wanted to see the paper I had written as a child. She'd found it fascinating the last time she was in here, but for that matter, so had Lily. Sure enough, she stopped right in front of it, leaning forward. I imagined her breath smudging the glass frame. I really needed to get rid of that thing; anyone that came in here seemed to be obsessed by it.

She turned toward me, the same compassion and sympathy evident that I had seen before. I watched as she made her slow approach, the draw of her beauty and sex appeal at odds with my revulsion toward the pity I saw in her eyes. I swore under my breath, determined to stay focused.

"You're sexy when you're working out."

"You're sexy all the time," I said, breathing hard.

"That was something, seeing the two of you at work. Shows me that what I saw before was you pretty much playing around. This was seriously impressive."

"Hadn't done rings since my accident."

"So that was your big comeback?"

"In a sense."

"I feel honored to–"

"Oh, no you don't." Sam was back with his ice pack. "Listen, Faith, if you can't leave him alone during *my* time, I'll make sure this becomes a closed practice. Xander has to pay attention. You can have him back the whole rest of the day after I'm done."

"She's not distracting me, Sam. It's okay. I swear."

"Are you two playing poker tonight?" she asked him.

"Well, *I* am," Sam said. "I learned a long time ago not to speak for this one. He's too unpredictable."

"Untamable," I corrected.

"Whatever you want to call yourself, X. Fifteen more minutes."

I nodded, content to keep running. Once I'd found my stride I could disconnect and think about anything. Well, almost anything. Normally when on the treadmill, I used headphones and ran to music, but I had rushed down the stairs so fast I hadn't had time to grab my iPod.

"If I make it at all, I'll be late," she said, watching me. "I have a show tonight."

"Show?" Sam assessed her. "You two meet at a strip joint?"

"Fuck off," I growled. "I already hit you once today, asshole."

"Only kidding, I swear." Sam held up his hands. He turned back to Faith. "What kind of show?"

"Dinner theater. You thought I was a stripper?" Faith laughed, flipping her hair over her shoulder.

"Well, you have the body for one." Sam glanced at me, a wicked gleam in his eye.

I knew what he was doing. He was trying to goad me into getting angry, into losing focus. Testing me.

"Strippers are way thinner than me!" Faith was still laughing.

"Depends on the place. Your curves are–"

"Stop checking her out," I snapped. "I know what you're doing."

"That so?"

"Yes. Stop." Enough was fucking enough. "Faith, I'll be done soon. Why don't you wait over there? Leave the dirty old man alone."

Faith hesitated, glancing between the two of us.

"Please, Faith."

She nodded, then returned to the bench on the opposite side of the room. Sam stepped closer.

"I wasn't making a play for your girl," he muttered.

"I know. You were testing me. I still didn't like it."

Sam looked at the glowing console in front of me. "Slow it down. You're already over four miles and you've only been running twenty minutes. Start your cooldown. We'll go to the free weights when time's up. How are you holding up?"

"Stop fussing."

"Then give me a straight answer."

"I'm fine. Other than adding rings, it's the same as yesterday."

"Rings take a lot out of you. You know that. Plus, it's been months."

"I was born for rings."

"Certainly seems that way sometimes. That's why it surprised me so much when you fell."

"Stupid mistake. Won't happen again."

"I certainly hope not. You've given me your word, after all."

A glance at the console told me I'd run another third of a mile.

"I don't know what came over me, Sam. I know how to fall."

"You know what came over you."

"I fucked everything up."

"Yep."

"Thanks."

"Hey, I'm not going to sugarcoat it. You were practically a sure bet for the next Olympics. For the third time. Now, not a chance. Your goal now is to make sure people remember you and recognize you as a fighter."

"Why would the sponsors want to pay for that?"

"Because logistically you still have a shot. It's not a good one. It's a snowball's chance in hell, actually, but it's still a shot. I'm going to play off that when I present to them. Don't focus on those chances. I'm going to have *them* focus on that, but *you* are to focus on doing your best and on giving the world a show. Don't hide. At this point in your career, you'll be thirty-three before the next Olympic Games. Don't kid yourself. There aren't that many gymnasts in their thirties. You would have been twenty-nine for this one. It's unlikely that you'll make it to the one after that. The clock is ticking. Milk the time you have left for all it's worth."

"Pastorini and Demanet were both in their forties, and they took home gold."

Sam barked a short laugh. "Pastorini and Demanet were both competing in the 'twenties! Ancient history. This is an entirely different game now, a young man's game, and you know it. Though, I admit that if anyone could pull it off, it would be you." His face darkened. "At least, at one time I believed that."

"Stop being so negative."

"You should be lifting. Get a move on. I'm not negative, I'm being realistic. Time will tell."

"I wish people would stop saying that."

Lifting went well and time sped by. Sam seemed pleased with my progress so far, anyway, and in what seemed like no time, he was bidding Faith and me goodbye.

I lifted one of my feet onto the pommel horse, stretching forward into a leaning split. I reached forward and grabbed my foot, then repeated the action with the other leg.

Faith never moved, just kept her eyes locked on me. I liked how it felt when she watched me. I made a bigger show of doing stretches than I otherwise would have.

"You can come over here. I won't bite," I called.

She walked over, a mischievous smirk on her face. "Actually, I recall you did bite me several times last night."

"Mmm… I'd like to bite you again."

"I'd like that, too." Her husky voice spoke directly to my libido. I took a deep, steadying breath and switched position, continuing to stretch. "What are you doing now?"

"Cooling off. Stretching again. Making sure my muscles don't get tight after the workout." I glanced down at the sweat that still glistened on my skin. "I need to take a shower. I'm sure I reek."

"Yes. But I love how you smell. It's so… macho."

"Macho!" I laughed.

"Masculine? Maybe I used the wrong word, but it's incredibly hot."

"I'll show you masculine. Come with me." She took my offered hand.

"Where?"

"I told you. I need a shower. Take one with me." I led her through the doors and into the kitchen to grab a bottle of water. Pausing, I gave her a quick kiss on the forehead. "I love how you smell, too. Like cherry blossoms. Drives me crazy. Whatever it is you use to make you smell like that, I'm going to have to pick it up by the gross."

Once in my bathroom upstairs, I turned on the shower and dropped my sweaty pants and boxers in the hamper. I grinned at Faith. "Strip for me."

She looked marginally surprised, then started to lift her shirt over her head.

"Wait," I said. "Do it slowly. Excite me."

Faith gave a pointed glance at my already semi-erect cock. "You seem to be getting pretty excited already."

My dick pulsed, hardening further under her gaze. I grinned. "That may be, but it's only because I know how this will end up. Doesn't mean I'm not interested in the floor show."

"Do you scare women with that thing?" she said, an appraising look on her face.

"Ha!" I chuckled. "I know better than to answer a question like that right now. Come on, Faith. Strip for me."

Faith hesitated, then turned her back on me. I crossed my arms and watched, curious what she had planned.

She kicked off her shoes. A moment later, she shimmied her hips in a provocative way as she allowed her jeans to slide down her long, beautiful legs. She cocked one hip up as she balanced all her weight on one foot and, *fuck me,* bent all the way over. I had a sudden image of walking up behind her and grinding myself against her sweet ass. The vision was so real, and it was all I could do to not act on it. Expending a huge amount of effort, I managed to restrain myself and remained unmoving, watching her.

She removed her pants and stood, arching her back forward and flipping her long hair back as she rose. Slowly, seductively, she crossed her arms in front at the hem of her shirt, then lifted it off in one fluid move. Now she stood before me in nothing but her matching black lace bra and panties. She reached behind her to unsnap her bra, but I crossed the room to her in a few fast strides. Pulling her back against me, I marveled at how perfectly we lined up like this. I pressed my cock between her legs and thrust, not penetrating her, but teasing. My tongue traced the outside of her ear, thrilling in her soft gasp when I nibbled on her earlobe.

"Do you want me, Faith?"

She merely nodded.

I grinned, kissing her neck. "I think you *do* want me. Know how I know?"

"How?"

I inhaled deeply. "I can smell your desire. And... the faint hint of cherries. I also know because when I do this," I thrust between her legs again, smirking as she–predictably–pushed back against me, "you respond in kind."

"Anything else?"

"Your voice is breathy when you're turned on. Like now. So sexy. And your eyes gleam, bringing out their brilliant color."

She stepped clear of me before turning around. I caught my breath as she gazed up at me. "Are they gleaming?"

I swallowed, my mouth suddenly parched. "Yes. They are." The last word was barely a whisper. Her face lit up, and she quickly removed her bra and panties.

Faith stood in front of me, naked and unashamed. I watched her, transfixed, as she reached for me and grabbed my cock. My breath whistled out through my teeth. Her soft hand stroked me, squeezed me, while her green eyes stared directly into my soul.

"I want to taste you."

I came back to myself with a start. "No. Not now. Shower."

"I want to taste you in the shower."

"Mmm… I think I want that, too."

I stepped away and into the stream of hot water. Faith stepped in after me and grabbed my hair, tugging me down to kiss her.

Her other hand slipped around my cock. Lubricated by the soap and water, she stroked from my balls up to the tip and back again, carefully running her fingers over the sensitive head as she did so. I moaned and thrust my hips forward.

When she released me, I felt a sense of loss. I wanted–needed–her to keep touching me. Stepping under the water, I rinsed off before I switched places with Faith so she was under the stream.

I squirted soap onto my hand and worked it into a lather before setting to work cleaning her. I took extra time cleaning her breasts because, after all, I needed to make sure they were squeaky clean. I lathered up her arms and stomach, then gently between her legs and down.

"My turn to wash you," she said, her voice husky as I stood back up.

I handed her the bottle, and she quickly poured some out, lathering up my chest, down to my stomach, and onto my hips and legs.

"Oh dear... will you look at that?"

"Hmm?"

"I see something else that still needs attention, too."

Good. "Is that so?"

Then her hands were kneading my balls, rolling and squeezing them between her fingers. I smacked my hand against the wall, allowing it to support my weight. "Shit! Faith..." I rasped.

"Shh... I've got you." Her lips closed with feathery-softness over the tip of my cock. I leaned my head back onto the hard tiled wall, completely lost. Her hand fisted the base as she rolled her lips over her teeth, sheathing them. Slowly, painstakingly, she took more and more of me into her mouth. Her tongue swirled around my dick, stroking me, teasing me. I yelled out a garbled groan as I felt myself press against the back of her throat. She answered me with a moan of her own, the vibrations shooting from the sensitive skin, all throughout my entire body.

A moan escaped my lips as she started to pick up speed. Her hand squeezed the base as she sucked me deep into her mouth, faster and faster. She was so beautiful, there on her knees, my cock in her mouth. I wanted to watch her work me into a frenzy, but my eyes squeezed shut on their own volition, only to fly open again as her other hand cupped my balls, applying pressure to the spot just beneath them.

"*Shit!* Oh my God, Faith! Stop… stop now, or I'm gonna come!" I gasped. I hadn't planned to come in her mouth, but the feeling hit me too fast and I was powerless to stop it. My words only seemed to spur her on, though, and instead of stopping, she sucked me even harder. Her tongue skated along the vein underneath. I looked down to see her eyes closed but crinkled as if she really enjoyed this, her head bobbing up and down.

Then she hummed again and my entire body tingled in that split second before my climax overtook me, emptying my balls and pent-up desire into the back of her throat. I leaned heavily on the wall, gasping for breath. Faith swallowed every drop, her tongue coming up and squeezing my dick into the roof of her mouth with each gulp.

"Christ, Faith. I love you."

She stood and caressed my face with her hand, cupping my cheek. "Do you really mean that? You said it last night, too. We've only been together less than twelve hours."

I hesitated, trying to wrap my mind around my own feelings. "Hmm. That may be, but I've missed you since the first time I laid eyes on you. I think I'd miss you even if we'd never met."

"That's… such a romantic thing to say."

"It's true, too." I smiled at her.

"How can it be?" She turned off the shower and stepped out, tracking water across the bathroom as she hunted for the towels. I hurried after her and grabbed one, holding it out for her. "All this is just… just *new*. We're like a drug to each other and we can't wait for our next hit. How can you say that it's love?"

"Because I've never felt like *this.*" I grabbed her hand and held it to my chest. "Not with anyone else, not ever. Come on, Faith. You feel it, too. You feel it when we touch, when we kiss, when we fuck. You feel our connection even when we aren't touching at all, just like I do. Admit it. This isn't a drug, it's the real thing. You know, you once said that maybe I'd been waiting for the right person all along. I think you were right. I had been waiting for *you* all that time."

She launched herself at me. I caught her, picking her up and throwing her over my shoulder. I slapped her ass and she squealed, slapping mine in retribution to lesser effect. I chuckled and carried her into my bedroom and deposited her on the bed.

"I think I owe you an orgasm or six." I laughed when her eyes got big and round. "Don't worry. You're in good hands."

CHAPTER THIRTEEN

We lay together, sated, her head on my chest and her shoulder tucked under my arm. Faith's fingers traced designs in my chest hair and tickled my skin. I caught her hand in mine and kissed it, content.

"I'm going to need to leave soon. I need to see Jacob, preferably before my show tonight."

I winced. This is what she chose to say to me right after we'd had mind-blowing sex? "Why?"

"I have to tell him it's over."

"Tell him over the phone."

Faith sat up and leaned over me, glaring. "I will not tell him over the phone. We've been together for a year. He deserves for me to tell him in person."

"He just told you yesterday that he loved you. He won't take it well. I don't want you alone with him for that. I'll go with you."

"You'll… what?" She gawked. "I don't think that's a good idea."

"Why?"

"Because you're you, and he's him. And both of you will end up in the hospital."

I stroked her face. "I can take care of myself, Faith."

"But I really don't want there to be a fight over this. I'll take care of it."

I didn't like it. I would much rather do *anything* other than allow Faith to be alone with that guy. It irked me that there was nothing I could do to stop her. Certainly not this early on. I climbed out of bed and stalked into my closet to get dressed.

"Are you pouting?" Faith asked.

"Maybe."

"That's adorable. Come back and lay down with me."

"Thought you were leaving."

"I said soon, not now."

"Are you hungry? We haven't eaten all day, and we've been burning a lot of calories." I pulled on a clean pair of boxers, followed by jeans and a tight black t-shirt.

"Yes, I am. Come here, please." I could almost feel her visually undressing me once more. I padded, barefoot, back to her.

She wrapped her arms around me, her cheek pressed into my hip. "Don't worry about Jacob, okay? I just need to do this, then it'll be over."

I sighed. "Did you tell him you loved him back last night?"

She released me and turned away, but not before I saw the shame etched on her delicate features. Shame... and guilt.

Did she love him? Was I doing her a disservice by chasing her? Was she just afraid of hurting my feelings? I grabbed socks from my dresser and tugged them on.

She still wasn't looking at me. Not a good sign. I slipped into my running shoes, kissed her on the top of her head, and headed downstairs to find food.

I glanced at the time. Nearly two. I shook my head. The look she'd had on her face cut me deeply. What was I going to do? Should I let her go?

Even as the thought crossed my mind, I knew I was crazy. How could I ever let her go now?

It was bad enough when Lily left me. We weren't a good match. Our entire "relationship" had been all about sex. Still, I'd let her in, and I was sure that was why I'd had anxiety attacks when any other woman looked at me. I didn't want to get hurt again. I mean, I was no shrink, but I was still damned sure that had something to do with it.

Faith was different. Sex with her was incredible and intimate, for sure, but our relationship was about far more. Her smile brightened my moods. I wanted to hear her sing, to take her to restaurants and movies. I wanted to date her, to wake up next to her and sleep with her by my side. I wanted her to be mine in every way, but even more than that,

I wanted to be hers. I wanted to show her the world. How could that be wrong when everything about her just felt right?

Everything except this: she was truly the woman of my dreams, but she didn't feel the same way about me. She had confessed her love for Jacob when she couldn't utter those words to me. That's what hurt. Was it unfair that I felt this way? Hell, yeah… but that didn't change anything. We'd only come to know each other these last five weeks, only been together for a day… but I'd wanted her for more than a year–ever since the first time we'd met. She'd sounded so happy on the phone last night… and I'd taken that away from her.

I rifled through my fridge, putting together the ingredients to make French bread pizza. This would work. Hopefully Faith *liked* pizza. Didn't most people? I heard her making her way down the stairs and knew she'd be joining me in a moment.

Arms wrapped around my waist, and her soft body pressed against my back. I laughed as she teasingly thrust her hips into my ass. I turned around. "I think you lack the proper equipment for that."

"I think you wouldn't be pleased if I had the proper equipment."

"You're right about that. Do you like pizza?"

"Who doesn't?"

"Good point." I popped them in the oven.

"I had no idea you were so domestic."

I chuckled. "Domestic? Not really. I'm just used to living alone. I have a cleaning lady who comes in once every other week to do all the shit I don't want to do, but other than that I just straighten as I go. As for cooking, I've learned how to make a few meals. I'm not really that picky about food."

"This is greasier than I would have expected from an athlete."

"I eat what I want, well… within reason. I tend to avoid most of the processed junk, but other than that, I burn it off so fast I have to eat high calorie foods."

"Interesting."

I reached out and traced her bottom lip with my thumb, then pulled her into my arms. I rested my cheek on the top of her head. "Did you call him yet?"

"Who?"

"Right answer."

"Oh. *Him.* No. I guess I should so I can make sure he can meet me."

"You sure I can't talk you into just doing it over the phone?"

"Would you like it if someone did that to you?"

I winced. "Lily broke up with me in person. Ripped my heart out and stomped on it. Then she did worse to me over the phone… but I already told you all that. To be honest, yes, I would have rather she'd just done it all over the phone. I'd rather not have given her the satisfaction of letting her see how much she'd hurt me."

Faith paled. "I hadn't thought about that."

"Just don't do it via text," I joked. "Faith, listen…"

"Yes?"

"Are you sure this is what you want?"

She looked confused as she gazed up at me. "This? You mean *us*?"

I didn't answer, just continued to watch her.

"Why would you think this isn't what I want?"

"Do you love him?"

"No!"

"But you said you did."

"I didn't know *what* to say. I didn't want to hurt him!"

"Maybe you didn't want to hurt him, but you sure seemed pretty excited about it last night."

"I …"

I turned away and grabbed a hot pad to remove the pizzas from the oven. The delicious smell filled the room and my stomach grumbled. I'd skipped breakfast because we had overslept, and now I thought I might die of starvation.

"Xander!" Faith snarled my name, her exasperation obvious.

"Yes?"

"I get what this is about, you know."

"Come and eat."

"This isn't over."

The corners of my mouth turned up in a sad smile I knew full well didn't reach my eyes. I slid the French bread pizzas onto plates and handed her one. "Beer?"

"Water, please. I don't like beer."

I grabbed the drinks and followed her to the table in an alcove off my kitchen.

"Xander, this is because I didn't say it back, isn't it?"

"Since you mention it, you said it to him even though you supposedly didn't mean it, but you can't say it to me. That's all." *Jesus Christ! Was that out loud?* Even I was blown away by how lame that sounded. "Also …"

"Xander…"

"Hear me out, Faith. I need to know that you're here because you *want* to be. Like I said, you sounded so happy on the phone last night. Now you're telling me that you don't love him, but you were *happy* last night. I worry that I took that from you."

"Look at me."

I blew on my pizza to cool it, then took a bite.

"Please, Xander. Look at me."

I did as she asked, our gazes locking. My pulse sped and my breath hitched. This was the effect she had on me. I couldn't take it. It had to stop. I'd tell her now that I couldn't do this, before I got any more attached.

"Faith, I–"

"No. Let me talk. Xander, when I interviewed you I was insanely attracted to you. I think you knew that. You made a joke of it. Remember? I couldn't concentrate. It was all I could do to not contact you again for a follow-up interview, just for the chance to see you again. When I emailed you the article I'd written, I hoped you'd suggest seeing me… but you didn't. I learned to accept it. You were out of my reach." She smiled wistfully. "I was just an awkward twenty-year-old, a college student crushing on the famous athlete way out of her league. I met Jacob and he was nice to me. I settled, realizing my dreams were out of the realm of possibility. Then I ran into you again at the *League.* I wanted so badly for you to kiss me that night, but you left. I followed you around, spent as much time as I could with you, content to be at least friends. One day I'd be able to tell my grandkids I was once friends with Orlando's most famous gymnast. When I called you last night, I could hear your pain and I knew I was making a huge mistake. I had to come here, and it was the best decision I could have made."

I reached out and took her hand, unable to bear the distance between us any longer. She looked at our entwined fingers and smiled.

"Xander, my mind tells me we haven't known each other long enough, but my soul feels like it's found its other half. I can't stand that you don't realize how I feel. I said I'd drop Jacob for a chance with you because you *are* what I want. I want you to know that I'm saying this because it's what I feel. I'm not just throwing around meaningless words to humor you or sooth your ego. I love you, Xander. It's crazy and irrational, but I do."

My breath caught in my throat. For a moment I was frozen. Then I reached out and stroked her cheek with my thumb. "Faith, you've made me so happy."

"I'm happy, too. Will you meet me tonight after my show? Oh wait… you have cards tonight. Never mind." She puckered for a kiss which I happily gave her.

"Nothing could keep me away from you tonight."

"No. You should go. Don't worry about me."

"I'll let you in on a secret. Those guys are great, but they don't hold a candle to you. Plus, my chances of sex are much higher hanging out with you." I smirked.

Her eyebrow arched in challenge. "So you're saying you only love me for my body?" She jabbed me in the chest with her index finger.

"Actually…" I caressed her cheek, letting my hand drift up to her temple. "I love your mind. It was your spirit that touched me that first night." My hand lowered, down her neck and onto her chest. "I love this, too. Your heart. Your passion. I loved hearing you sing and hope to do that again, and soon. I love your courage, that you came here in the middle of the night just because you felt I needed you. I *did* need you, Faith. In every way. Also," I grinned, "your body is a nice fringe benefit."

My stomach growled loudly, killing the moment. "Come on. Let's eat. Then I'll have you for dessert."

"I still need to call Jacob."

I nodded. "Okay. After we eat. Then I'll console you." I shoved a huge bite in my mouth.

"You have a one-track mind!"

"Right now I do, yep. Eating."

Faith laughed and dug into her own food.

After the last bite had been eaten, Faith pulled out her phone and checked the time. With a huge sigh, she tapped the screen and placed the call. I collected our dishes and stepped into the kitchen to rinse them. I was still close enough to see and hear her, but far enough to appear respectful and, with the water running, give the appearance of not eavesdropping.

"Um… hi, Jacob. It's Faith. Listen, I need to talk to you. Give me a call when you get this message, okay? Bye."

"He didn't answer." Faith was at my side in a moment. She pointed to the dirty dishes. "I can do that."

"I've got it. I was just staying busy so I didn't hover during your phone call." I shut off the water. "What time do you need to go so you can get ready for your show?"

"We have warm-ups and go over any notes at five. I need to go home and change and get my stuff before that, though. I'd say I have about an hour. What did you have in mind?"

"Oh, I have a few ideas. First, though, I have to ask you a question." I assumed a completely serious expression.

"What's that?"

"Will you go out on a date with me?"

Faith burst into laughter and smacked me in the chest. "You scared me! You looked so serious."

"I am serious."

"Yes, goofy, I will go out on a date with you."

"How's tomorrow?"

"Hmm… tomorrow is no good. I have another show. Sunday is the one day I don't have a show or work right now, but I have to get up early the next day. How about Thursday?"

"Thursday it is. Eight?"

"I'm off at six-thirty, so that works perfectly."

"Good."

"What's your schedule like, in general?" she asked.

"To be honest, I'm not sure. Sam has it in his head that it would be a good idea for me to get back into the competition circuits. I'm so far behind, though. I have no chance of making the Olympic team. Besides, I've lost my edge. It'll be a lot of hard work, and I suspect Sam is going easy on me until my next MRI.

"Events could be anywhere in the world, assuming my sponsors give me the green light, which I doubt. Sam thinks they will, though, and he could sell snow to an Eskimo. I would be gone for days at a time. Even when I'm here, my schedule can get pretty brutal. And there's the issue of the press. They are everywhere. People who'll try to find dirt on each of us to feed their readers' curiosity. People who will make up lies because it's provocative. Are you sure you're up to this?"

Hell, I was already dreading some of that. Competing in other countries without her with me sounded like torture and it wasn't even on the radar yet.

Faith bit her lip. "Comes with the territory, I suppose. Reporters don't scare me. I used to be one. Will you miss me when you travel?"

"Of course I will." In fact, the more I thought about it, I'd love to bring her with me to some of my events. But I stayed silent, afraid to overwhelm her more than I likely already had.

A *ping* like the sound of a crystal bell rang out and startled us both. Faith grabbed her phone and swiped the screen, paling almost immediately. She held her phone out to me.

From: Jacob A.

Incoming text: Two-timing bitch! I know everything. How could you?

Fuck! What new hell is this?

CHAPTER FOURTEEN

I turned on my heel and charged out the front door. I stopped at Faith's car, placing my hand on the roof. I searched in every direction. I saw no sign of anything out of place, but the tree line at the edge of my property obscured my visibility.

"How would he know? I never told anyone I was coming here." Faith had followed me outside. Worry and nervousness marred her beautiful face.

"What does Jacob do?"

"He's just a security guard for some agency."

"What?"

"You know, overnight guard for a car dealer, backup mall security, school security, directs traffic for big events, or occasionally even a bodyguard for hire. That sort of thing."

"Rent-a-cop?"

"Yeah, exactly. He hates that term, though."

A cold chill went down my spine as I was overwhelmed by the sensation that we were being watched. "He carry a gun?"

She shook her head. "No. Never. The company never allows it, and he doesn't know how to use one, anyway."

Good. "Okay. Let's get back inside."

"Do you think he knows we're here?"

"Looks that way."

I locked the door behind us. Running my hands through my hair, I tried to collect my thoughts. Okay… Faith hadn't told anyone, that much was obvious. She'd been with me the entire time. That meant that bastard had to have tracked her here. He'd probably stuck something on either her car or—more likely—her phone. That sounded like something a rent-a-cop would do.

The sound of a dialing phone made my head whip toward Faith. "What are you doing?"

She held up her index finger and hit the speaker button. I heard a clicking sound.

"The fuck do you want, bitch?" Jacob snarled.

I opened my mouth, but a glare from Faith kept me silent.

"Jacob, what are you talking about?" she asked.

"You know very well what I'm talking about. I know where you are, and I know who you're with. You're nothing but a slut! Did you tell him you loved him, too?"

"That's enough!" I roared. "You will *not* speak to her that way." I grabbed for the phone, but Faith pulled it out of my reach and turned her back. My hands clenched hard into fists. My body vibrated with the intensity of my fury.

"Phoenix! I fucking knew it!" His tone became threatening. *"You'd better hope I never see you, asshole. You'll both be sorry."*

The line went dead.

Why was my life never dull? Seriously, between crazy people drugging Lily over a job and Faith's ex-boyfriend threatening me, I had enough material to write a book.

"You shouldn't have done that," said Faith.

"Get him back on the phone!"

"Xander…"

"Get him back on the fucking phone, Faith."

"Xander, he's not going to pick up. Not after that display. You shouldn't have said anything. It only pissed him off more."

I closed my eyes and silently counted to ten. She was right, but I *hated* to admit it. No use in making a bad situation worse, anyway.

The sound of the front door opening forced my eyes open. "Faith! Wait… where are you going? *Why* are you going?"

"I have to get home and get ready… and I need time to think."

I stepped closer, almost touching her. "To think?"

"Yes," she whispered.

"About what?"

"Us. You, Jacob. That insane testosterone-induced fight."

"I wasn't going to let him talk to you like that, Faith. Why are you so pissed over that?"

"I told you I wanted to handle it. I didn't need or want your help. I'm not some helpless girl, Xander. I can take care of myself. Anyway, it's a lot to process right now. I need to be alone."

My heart pounded. This was it. She wanted to think about *us* and whether she could stand my hotheaded temper and mouth. I couldn't force her to give us a chance if she didn't want to. I shut the door, trapping her between me and it, and inhaled deeply, breathing in her scent. I placed my hands on the door on either side of her head, careful not to touch her. "I'll miss you, baby," I whispered. "I'll still see you tonight?"

"Yes."

"I don't want you to leave. He obviously tracked you here. He could be watching for you."

"I don't think he'd do anything stupid. He'd get caught and he knows it. Especially after what he just said on the phone. Look..." Faith sighed. "Jacob is a good guy. He's not violent or manipulative. I don't know how he found out I was here, but he wouldn't do anything to hurt anyone. I'm positive of that."

I didn't move, I simply stood stock still and gazed into her mesmerizing green eyes. I was so close I could feel her warmth heating me, teasing me. I hummed low in my throat, and the effect on her was instantaneous. Her eyes darkened and her lips parted as her breathing came faster. Her tongue snaked out to moisten her lips and I found myself staring. The desire to kiss her was overwhelming. There was something shadowing the depths of her eyes, though.

Anxiety… and arousal. She was every bit as affected by my proximity as I was by hers. That much was obvious. That said, I could tell she wanted me to let her leave, hoped I would respect her wishes. Her eyes begged me to understand. Every instinct I had urged me to convince her to stay… but she *wanted* to go. Even after what Jacob had said, she trusted him. That should be enough for me. I wanted her to be happy, and I wanted her to trust *me* like that.

I cleared my throat. "Better be a good girl and run along home now, before I consider making you stay."

She trembled but nodded, relieved. Slowly I backed away and gave her space. With a trembling hand, she opened the door and scurried out. I watched her climb into her car and drive away, then shut and locked the door.

She may have said she needed to think about us, but her body's reaction to me told me I was still in this game.

I went upstairs and powered on my laptop to purchase a ticket to Faith's show, then checked my email. Even though I'd told her I'd meet her after the show, I'd actually enjoyed the play the first time and wanted to see it again. Her passion drew me in, not only in the bedroom, but when she performed. It was important to her. That made it important to me, and I wanted to support her dreams, whatever form they came in.

My back had started to feel stiff after everything today, so I wandered into the bathroom and filled the large Jacuzzi tub with hot water, stripped, and climbed in. It seemed as good a way as any to pass the time.

The house felt strangely empty without Faith in it. So much had happened in the last twenty-four hours. I thought over everything since she'd called me the night before, thought back to all the encounters we'd ever had. Hard to believe things had finally played out this way. I was a lucky bastard, and she was worth waiting for.

The sound of footsteps downstairs sent all my senses on high alert. My ears strained, listening. Everything was silent now, but I was sure I'd heard it. I climbed out of the tub, wrapping a towel around my waist before I set off down the stairs.

I found no one in the living room or kitchen, no one in the guest room or downstairs bathroom. I flung open the double doors to my gym, scrutinizing every inch of the place.

"Hello?" I yelled, my voice carrying through the silent house. No response. I must have been hearing things.

I walked out of the gym and saw something that made my blood run cold and set every hair on the back of my neck on end.

The front door wasn't closed all the way. I distinctly remembered shutting and locking that when Faith had gone.

"You'll both be sorry!" Jacob's words echoed in my brain. What did he have planned? I flung open the door the rest of the way and stepped out, feeling goosebumps travel across my chest and arms. No one here. I watched an old Chevy truck turn off this street onto the next, but nothing appeared out of the ordinary.

I began to doubt my own memory. Had I really locked that door? Maybe it just hadn't latched all the way. I turned back and jiggled the handle; unlocked. Well, maybe I'd misremembered that, too. To be on the safe side, I carefully locked the door behind me and searched my whole house again. No one was here. Nothing seemed out of place.

Weird.

I'd never felt so exposed in my own home before. I didn't like it. "Just so you know, I have a gun. I *will* shoot any intruders on sight."

No response.

I shook my head, feeling foolish. Now, not only was I talking to no one, I was *lying* to no one as well. My buddy John had often tried to take me shooting with him, but I'd never gotten around to it. It's not that I didn't like guns, they were just a hobby I didn't have time for.

A glance at the clock informed me that it was half past five. I wanted to be at the theater early, probably by six-thirty, and it was half an hour away. I needed to get ready.

Goosebumps covered my damp flesh. I could almost *feel* eyes on me as I ascended the stairs. Was it just my overactive imagination?

CHAPTER FIFTEEN

The auditorium was dimly lit, the stage dark. Patrons were already assembling and finding their tables or perusing the menus as the orchestra began warming up. I picked mine up and scanned the wine selections.

"Are you ready to order, sir?"

I glanced at the gum-chewing waitress. With as much effort as this place had made to make the menus and general ambience seem classy, you'd think it would be against policy to snap gum like that.

"Uh, yes. I'll have a glass of the Pinot Noir," I absently pointed at the entry, "and an order of the pan-seared Atlantic salmon."

"You got it. I'll be right back with your drink." With a final pop, she was off to check on another table.

I skimmed the program until I got to the actor biographies, and read Faith's section as if trying to commit it to memory. I should have brought flowers again. I shook my head at my thoughtlessness. I checked my phone to make sure it was silenced. Fifteen minutes to show time. I shifted in my seat, glancing around for the waitress.

I caught a whiff of a weird burning smell and scowled. That didn't bode well for my meal.

The room took on a slight haze, and the smell became stronger. A woman at a nearby table made a nasty comment about the cook and coughed overdramatically.

Then the fire alarms went off. I jumped to my feet as the sprinklers doused the room in freezing cold water. Several women screamed and ran for the door. Orchestra members leapt to their feet and attempted to keep their precious instruments dry as they ran for the exit and the backstage doors. The waitresses all walked out of the kitchen carrying wine glasses and bottles, confused expressions on their faces.

One look at the wait staff told me that this wasn't a kitchen fire.

I took off at a run toward the backstage area and burst through the door, working my way through the crowd of people. The smell of smoke filled the air and burned my sinuses. Not far from me, people hurried through the open loading dock door. Somewhere nearby a woman cried. Men shouted to each other as they tried to organize the evacuation efforts.

"Excuse me, sir, you can't be back here now," a tall security guard yelled when he caught sight of me, barely understandable over the ear-splitting sound of the alarm. "The fire department is already on its way. Most people are clear. Only the dressing room is affected. Please leave through the front doors with the rest of the patrons."

"I have to find my girlfriend. I can take care of myself. I'll just fall in with the crowd."

"Mr. Phoenix, I told you to get the fuck out of here."

The familiar sound of his menacing tone immediately demanded my attention. *Jacob!*

"Where is Faith?" I demanded.

His expression seemed to soften, even if only a little. "I don't know."

"The fuck you don't!"

"I think she got out. I haven't seen her. Now please let me do my job. I need to escort all guests– including you–off the premises."

"Not until I find her." I started to walk past him, but he jabbed his finger in my chest.

"Right now, I'd love nothing more than to beat the shit out of you, but I have to get everyone to safety, and that, unfortunately, includes you. Now move!"

"Not a chance." I ran past him, ducking under his arm. I made it to the loading dock and turned to look behind me, but Jacob was gone.

I stepped outside. "Faith!"

My eyes darted from person to person, finally falling on the crying woman. It was the girl who had thought I was Jacob the last time I had been here. Weird that she had mistaken us when he apparently worked as a guard here. Two large steps carried me to her. "Have you seen Faith?"

Her only response was to cry harder and point back into the building. I turned to look but had no idea what she was trying to tell me.

"Listen, I have to find her. Tell me what happened!"

"I don't know! There was smoke, so much smoke. We didn't know where it was coming from. It was hot, but it's always hot back there. Nothing was on fire, we checked! I came out to the hall to see if it was out there, and… and…"

"And?"

Her eyes took on a haunted expression. "The ceiling in the dressing room collapsed. I couldn't see far inside, but I could hear the screaming. I–I ran."

Without hesitation, I turned and sprinted back into the building. I had to get in there. I had to hope she was okay.

I raced down the hall and turned the corner. I had only been in the dressing room briefly, but didn't remember any windows. That meant that most likely there had to be a second door or the fire marshal would have been all over this place. At least, I hoped so.

As described, charred, broken remains of huge props and set pieces blocked the door. I didn't know if I had time to move it all, especially with any possible help lost to the chaos. I decided I should keep looking. Black, ashy footprints on the floor leading from around the corner confirmed my suspicions.

My eyes and lungs burned from the smoke. I ripped the tail of my shirt, quickly tying the material around my nose and mouth as I hurried down the hall and around another corner. The other door was wide open and swinging outward, kicked free and dangling from a single hinge. Oppressive smoke and heat poured through the opening.

For a moment, I hesitated. The footprints and condition of the door told me the room's occupants had fled. I hadn't seen anyone outside covered in soot, though, and I certainly hadn't seen Faith.

I braced myself and stepped into Hell.

The room looked like a warzone. Smoke filled the space and the scream of the alarm was still deafening. Counters had been crushed, mirrors were shattered. Chairs were thrown around the room like so many children's toys, and the racks of clothing were completely destroyed. The ceiling had collapsed. The destruction was so chaotic the floor had been almost entirely obscured. Flames licked the broken beams and consumed every flammable item in its path.

I took a deep breath and immediately started coughing, gasping. It felt like there was no air left in here. I pressed forward, trying not to touch anything. When I had been in here last, I had entered through the other door. Faith had been to the far left, which should be the south side. I made my way over there, kicking rubble out of the way.

There was no one in here. Why would anyone have stayed? This was stupid; I should have kept looking outside. I struggled to breathe. My head spun, woozy from the lack of air. The heat seared my skin. With a last scan of the corner, I turned to leave.

Something in my peripheral vision made me pause. It was probably nothing, just a spare wig on the floor. Just in case, though, I stepped toward it and pulled. The black hair didn't budge. I knocked some debris away and found that the hair belonged to a girl, one of the actresses, I guessed. She lay face down on top of something. By sweeping her hair back, I could see burns covered her entire face, making her unrecognizable. I couldn't tell if she was dead or unconscious. Either way, I was getting us both out of here.

I tried to lift her from beneath her arms, but she wouldn't budge. Shit. A broken beam had come down on her legs. I set her down, trying to think of what to do next, when I saw a mass of soot-covered red hair.

It was Faith. This girl had fallen on top of Faith, her torso and various debris shielding Faith and blocking her from immediate view. Ignoring a wave of dizziness, I shoved away at more debris, scorching my hands. I had to get her out. I glanced at the other girl. I needed to get them both out of here... but how?

Please let Faith be okay. Please let them both be okay. A glance at the first girl's trapped legs told me I needed to get Faith out first... not that I had ever really considered otherwise. I yanked Faith free, scooped her into my arms, and stumbled for the door as fast as I could. The room felt like it had expanded; every step was an effort. I couldn't breathe, could barely see anymore. My vision swam.

No! I wouldn't, *couldn't,* give up. One step, then another. She was a deadweight in my arms, and I tried not to contemplate what that could mean. Another step, almost there.

I stumbled and almost fell. A few more steps and we were at the swinging door. I rushed through it and crashed into the wall on the other side, coughing. Had to keep going. Down the hall, then a left turn, toward the loading docks and fresh air.

I turned the corner and my vision dimmed. My ears sounded like they were underwater, quieting the screaming fire alarms. Several shadowy shapes ran toward me just as my knees buckled and I dropped to the floor.

"Another girl… dressing room… south wall," was all I could gasp out. I didn't recognize my own voice.

Everything went dark.

CHAPTER SIXTEEN

"This one's coming around."

Something cold pressed against my face. A sharp hissing sound filled the air. An oxygen mask... with some sort of funny bag attached to the bottom. I tried to sit up, but the mask pressed harder. The man holding it in place smiled at me.

"Easy, buddy. You're gonna be just fine. You were only out for about a minute." He was clean shaven with dark brown hair. He wore a black jacket with the words *Firefighter EMT* on it.

"Faith!" My voice was garbled and distorted.

"What?"

"Faith!"

"Are you asking about the girl you were carrying?"

I tried to nod, but again found myself impeded by the mask.

He shook his head and pointed to a nearby ambulance, where they were strapping Faith to a stretcher. "Over there, they're about to take her to the hospital."

"She's alive?" I had no idea how anyone was supposed to understand me with this thing on. I might as well have been speaking some other language.

Luckily, the guy seemed fluent in mask-language. "She's stable for the moment."

I snatched the mask away. "I have to go with her." I forced myself to sit up.

"No, *you* have to sit here and keep this mask on." I glared at him as he pushed it back onto my face.

"Don't look at me like that. We have two ambulances present, a couple more on the way. Your friend is going in that one, and firefighters have gone after the girl you said was still trapped inside. She gets the other. You'll be sent soon enough. You need to be monitored for a few hours."

I jerked the mask away again. "I want to be sent to wherever she's going."

"You keep that mask on. I'll personally make sure of it. Deal?"

I nodded.

He eyed me for a moment, then wandered off. I took stock of my situation. I was sitting on some sort of padded mat on the ground alongside a fire truck. My jacket and tie had been removed. People milled all around in a chaotic mess. Police officers tried to organize the crowd and take statements.

CHAPTER SIXTEEN

A lone firefighter emerged through the loading dock door, carrying the young woman I had seen inside. EMTs rushed over and took her. One grabbed her wrist and squeezed, then shook his head. They quickly strapped her to a stretcher that had been lowered to the ground and began chest compressions. I looked away, unable to watch anymore.

"You're the one who ran in there?" The voice startled me. I had been so intently watching the paramedics I hadn't noticed the officer approach. I nodded. "I'm Detective Bentley. Your name?"

"Alexander Phoenix." He cocked his head and frowned. I started to lower the mask to answer again.

"Don't even think about it!" Looked like my friend the paramedic had returned. I sighed and nodded apologetically to the detective.

"I need to ask him some questions," Bentley argued.

"That's fine. Ask away. But he needs to leave his mask on." He turned to me. "Not kidding, man. We had a deal."

"He can't understand me," I said.

The detective laughed. "I can understand you just fine. I was just trying to figure out where I'd heard your name before."

"Oh. I'm a gymnast. Olympian."

"I don't think that's it. I don't watch gymnastics. Anyway, Mr. Phoenix, can you tell me what happened?"

"I was here to watch my girlfriend perform in the show. Noticed smoke. Alarms and sprinklers went off. I went looking for her. The woman over there told me the fire started on the next floor and the ceiling collapsed in the dressing room. I went inside and found her and another girl. Tried to get them out."

"I'd say you did a good job getting them out," the paramedic interjected.

"Just one."

"You told the firefighters where the other one was. You may have saved her life. Don't beat yourself up." He looked over to where the other group of paramedics loaded her into the ambulance. I remembered the look on the EMT's face when he shook his head right before they started doing chest compressions, and I doubted that.

"Had you seen anything suspicious?" Bentley asked.

"No, I didn't see a–"

I froze. I looked around the dock in all directions. No sign of Jacob anywhere.

"Faith, you didn't tell me Jacob was coming! Come in, come in!"

"Um… he's not. He hates musicals"

She wouldn't have been so shocked had he really worked there.

"You'll both be sorry!"

"The guard…"

"Which one?"

"His name is Jacob Armistead. He was dressed as a security guard. I think he may have had something to do with it."

"Why?"

"He doesn't work here, but acted like he did tonight… and was in the backstage area. He tried to stop me from looking for my girlfriend. She and I only hooked up recently. They, Jacob and Faith, were together. He was outside my house today. Maybe inside, too. Threatened us."

"Threatened?"

"Nothing specific. Just said 'we'd be sorry.'"

"I see. Mr. Phoenix, do you have a contact number where you can be reached in case we have further questions?" The detective made some notes and asked me a few final questions, then continued on to the next person.

The crowd slowly dispersed, though several stragglers hung back to see how things played out. I saw no sign of Jacob anywhere.

"Looks like your ride is here." The paramedic pointed to another pair of ambulances turning the corner. "Ready to go?"

"What will happen?"

"Well, you inhaled a fair bit of smoke. They'll have you checked out by a pulmonologist and under observation for a few hours to make sure that you haven't inhaled too much carbon monoxide or other fumes. Assuming everything checks out, you'll be free to go. If it doesn't, they'll keep you there and on oxygen for a few days. You weren't unconscious long, so I think you'll be fine. In a couple of days your body should filter out all the toxins and you'll be good as new."

"What about Faith?"

"I didn't get a good look, but she had a good team looking after her. I know she had a pulse, and that's a good thing."

"Will they let me stay with her?"

"I'm sure. They won't update you on her condition, though, unless she wakes up and consents. Only family." The ambulances pulled up and stopped. The paramedic approached them and started an animated conversation, then walked over to rejoin me. He unhooked the oxygen tank from the truck and tucked it under his arm. "Come with me."

Feeling like I was on a leash, I dutifully stood up and followed after him. They directed me onto a stretcher, loaded me up into the ambulance, and we were off.

My mind travelled to thoughts of the burned girl receiving CPR. Had I freed her legs and gotten her out faster, would she have had a better chance? No telling.

Just like the night my sister had died. A single choice, a single *moment* in time, and lives are irreparably changed. How I'd wished I could have saved my sister that night. I had visited her friend often after the accident, right up until her death. I had seen her waste away. I had felt true helplessness.

Had I been able to repeat things, I would have done *so* many things differently. For starters, I would have done a better job being there for my sister, would have kept better tabs on her. I would have been a better brother. I would have made sure she was nowhere near a car that night, even if I'd had to sabotage the damned thing myself. But hindsight is *always* twenty-twenty.

Would I have chosen differently tonight? I considered the outcomes, but no. There was no way I would have carried Faith out of there second. If that meant I had essentially killed the other girl myself, I'd have to live with it. But I was getting ahead of myself. I had no reason to believe she hadn't made it.

"We're here." The ambulance pulled to a stop and the EMT shoved open the door. The driver emerged and together they carried me out on the stretcher.

"I can walk."

"Just following protocol. You'll stay there until hospital staff says otherwise."

The pair wheeled me in through the sliding doors and up to a tall counter. A woman in bright blue scrubs stood up and eyed me.

"Another from the theater fire," the EMT that had ridden in the back with me said.

"This one's awake," she observed.

"Awake and stable. Stats were good on the way here. Blood pressure normal, pulse ox reads ninety-eight. He's been on one-hundred-percent oxygen for the last twenty minutes. He did lose consciousness inside the building, but fire department paramedics tell me the episode was only around a minute."

She nodded and consulted her computer. "What's your name, sir?"

"Alexander Phoenix."

She nodded and tapped at her keys. "Go ahead and take him to room thirty-three."

"Wait!" I jerked the mask away from my face. She stopped and looked up at me. "There were two young women brought here before me. One of them a redhead named Faith Richardson. Is she okay?"

"There were women brought here before. No identification on either of them. You family?"

I shook my head. "I rescued Faith from the building. She's my g–my fiancée."

A beeping sound from a monitor on the side of the stretcher made the nurse frown. "You need to put your mask back on and calm down. I have no information at this time on either of the women. Room thirty-three, please," she snapped at the EMTs, who wheeled me down the hall.

The room was barely larger than a cubicle, separated by a clear glass sliding door. As soon as I was unstrapped, I slid off the stretcher and sat up on the emergency room bed.

"Should have gone with wife," the ambulance driver said.

"Excuse me?"

"She would have been more forthcoming if you'd have said wife. If you're going to lie, go big or go home."

"I wasn't lying."

He held his hands up in surrender. "Of course not. All I know is that ever since the movie *While*

You Were Sleeping, everyone and their brother has tried the fiancée bit. The hospital is a magical place full of sudden engagements. I should have realized yours was real, though. Your call button is here. Press it if you need assistance."

He unhooked my mask from the oxygen tank and connected it to a panel on the wall and flipped a switch. He picked up the tank, set it on the stretcher, and then both paramedics left.

I examined the claustrophobic's nightmare I was trapped inside, which took all of thirty seconds. The only furnishings in the room were the bed, a single chair, and a rolling table. Several weird-looking medical instruments were fastened to the wall, but that was it. A small computer monitor sat in a corner, silent and dark.

The slight hissing of the mask was the only sound that broke the silence. With no distractions, my mind wandered again to Faith. I hoped she was going to be okay. I would never forgive myself for not finding her faster if she wasn't. I wondered what time it was. I reached for my pocket to pull my phone out, but was startled by the stinging pain on the palms of my hands. I'd forgotten that I'd burned them in all the excitement. Rough callouses covered my palms and fingers from years of gymnastics. I should be thankful for them; they were the reason the blistering wasn't worse.

I swiped the screen to unlock my phone and sent a quick text to Sam letting him know where I was.

Predictably, the phone rang less than a minute later. I hit the speaker option.

"Phoenix."

"The fuck are you doing in the hospital?"

"Good to hear from you, too, Sam."

"Don't give me that shit. What happened?"

"Fire at the theater."

"You were stuck in a fire?"

"Not exactly. I ran into the burning room to try to help rescue, um, people."

"Jesus. You okay?"

"They keep telling me to keep the oxygen mask on, and my hands are a bit blistered, but I'm okay."

"You know, Xander, if you didn't want to compete anymore, all you had to do was say so."

"Very funny, asshole. Listen, Faith's here somewhere, too. I don't know if she's—"

"Why am I not surprised she was involved somehow?"

"Fuck, man. Stop that. I don't even know if she's alive right now. There was another girl trapped in there too, I... I don't know if she made it, either."

Sam's voice became muffled as he covered the phone to talk to whomever was in the room with him. "Sit tight. We're on our way."

The line went dead. *We?* Oh, right. Friday night poker. I glanced at the time. Only a little after eight o'clock. The night had dragged on forever. I put the mask down and stood up, stretching. I stuck my phone in my pocket and headed for the door to poke my head out.

"Get back in there and put your mask back on. I'll be with you in a minute," a passing nurse in blue scrubs snapped. She disappeared into another room, pushing a cart in front of her.

God damn it. I was fine. I didn't need the mask. What I needed was to find Faith. I stepped into the hallway and followed the nurse to the other room, standing just on the outside of the sliding glass door. I crossed my arms and glowered at her.

Noticing me, the nurse hurried out. "There a problem?"

"I'd say so. Everyone keeps telling me to put the fucking mask on, but no one wants to give me any answers."

"Come on." She led the way back to my room. "What questions do you need answered?"

"Where is my fiancée? I want to see her." The woman looked genuinely confused, so I continued.

"Long red hair, green eyes. She was brought here before me. Her name is Faith Richardson."

She shook her head, still looking confused or unsure.

"Look," I continued. "I know she's here. I pulled her out of the burning building myself. I feel I have a right to know where she is and to see her. Please, don't you understand? I love her. You let me see her, and I'll put the mask on and behave."

The woman looked sad. Without a word, she turned and shut the sliding glass door to my room. "I know who she is. The whole hospital heard about the fire and what you did. It was very brave of you to rescue her. She's not on this floor. Listen to me, you can see her later, but you have to stay here for observation for a little while. She's in the hyperbaric chamber for the next couple of hours, anyway. You can't get to her. Cooperate and let us do our jobs and keep an eye on you. I'll find out what room she is in and tell you when you're done here."

"Do you know anything about the other girl? The one with dark hair and burns everywhere? Her legs were trapped when the ceiling collapsed."

"Were you family?" Her voice and expression cooled instantly. Her body language told me she didn't want to discuss this.

I shook my head, opting for honesty. "I don't even know her name. She was with Faith in the room. I carried Faith out but collapsed. I told the firefighters she was in there before I blacked out. So much smoke…"

"I couldn't say, sir. Let me take your vitals. You'll need to put the mask back on. Someone will be in to take blood work in a little while."

The nurse pulled her cart into the room, placed a clip on my finger, then wrapped a cuff around my arm to take my blood pressure. After she'd left me alone to my own thoughts again, mask in place, I realized she had asked me if I *was* family… past tense. I wondered if the girl had even been alive when I'd found her in the room. Did I ever have a chance to save her? Despite my earlier thoughts about knowing I had made the right choice in getting Faith out first, I still felt remorseful. I laid back against the pillow and closed my eyes, resigned to do as I was told and wait for Sam and the doctor. *Then* I'd find Faith if I had to search every room of this hospital.

CHAPTER SEVENTEEN

The dim room soothed my frazzled nerves.

Faith's hair spread artfully across her pillow as she slept. I knew I should sleep, too, but I couldn't tear my eyes away from her.

I'd barely left Faith's side for an entire week. She'd had three therapy sessions in the hyperbaric chamber. They'd finally removed her oxygen mask after her final treatment, and I had hopes they would release her soon.

The press had camped out in the hospital parking lot. The one time I'd risked going out there was when the Emergency Room had discharged me. They had insisted on taking me outside in a wheelchair, despite my insistence that I wasn't going anywhere. Apparently, that was their policy.

As long as I was already out there, I had given in to Sam's suggestion that we go pick up my car. It had been left at the theater and, the way my luck had gone lately, it would have been towed before I got to it, otherwise.

I'd gone ahead and had my MRI on Monday to get Sam off my back. They were able to do it in this hospital, so I didn't even have to go anywhere, which was a major part of why I'd agreed. I hated those things; like being trapped inside the world's noisiest coffin.

Regardless of his early reservations about Faith, Sam had been a true friend through this ordeal. He went back and forth between my place and the hospital so I wouldn't have to contend with the media circus outside. Among other things, he brought me a few changes of clothes and some toiletries, as well as a small air mattress so I could stop sleeping sitting up.

Despite the horrible reason for being there, Faith and I grew even closer. With nothing to do to pass the time except talk and watch horrible daytime television, we chatted about anything and everything. Things that we probably never would have ever discussed outside this place became lengthy conversations. We had spirited debates. I now knew without a shadow of a doubt that my feelings for her ran much, *much* deeper than anything I had ever known.

We'd been interviewed again by Detective Bentley, the cop whom I'd spoken to outside the theater. Faith remained convinced that Jacob had not had anything to do with the fire, but had no explanation why he'd been there in the first place.

I glanced at the clock. Six in the morning. The sun would be up soon. Grabbing my laptop, I powered it on and pulled up an internet browser. Being cooped up in a hospital room meant that I'd been effectively cut off from the outside world. Thinking about the press outside made me wonder what was being said about the fire.

Typing the name of the theater into the search bar brought up several news articles. I read a few, scrolling further down the list.

I paused.

My hand shook as I enlarged a picture on the Times website. The image's focus was of me carrying Faith toward the loading dock. Damn, we looked a mess. But to the right there was a familiar yet blurry image of a blonde woman. Squinting, I realized it was Lily. Not all of her, but enough that I could definitely identify her.

What was she doing there? Why would she be in this picture? I stared at the photo, willing it to give me a clue. Finally, I dismissed it. Lily was a reporter. There was no reason she *shouldn't* be there. I was just glad that I hadn't seen her.

Lily's appearance in the same picture as me was unsettling. I closed the screen and set the computer aside.

I watched Faith sleep. I'd missed seeing her face unobscured by the mask, and now that it was gone, I couldn't get enough of looking at her.

A shrill beep startled me. Adrenaline coursed through my body and made my heart pound. Shit! That IV alarm was loud. I stood to hit Faith's call button when the nurse knocked on the door and entered.

"I knew that thing would need to get switched out soon," the night nurse said, way too perky for this early in the morning. I scowled and tried to calm my racing pulse.

"What time is it?" Faith said sleepily.

"Quarter to seven," said Nurse Perky. "I'll just change out this IV and be out of your way, unless you need anything."

Faith yawned, stretched. "No, I'm good. Thanks. Will I be able to go home today?"

"That's up to the doctor. I'll be leaving soon, and Ashlyn will be taking over as your nurse for the day. Have a good one."

Faith climbed out of bed and padded over to the bathroom. After answering nature's call, she wandered over to me and climbed into my lap. "Haven't you slept?"

"Wasn't tired."

"You have dark circles around your eyes, silly. What have you been doing?"

I shrugged. Oh well, not like I needed to hide my infatuation from the woman I loved. "Watching you."

179

"All night?"

"All night. I missed being able to see your face. You've been hiding behind a mask all week."

"Hiding?" She giggled. "Like I had a choice. Kiss me."

I stroked her bare cheek with the side of my thumb, then leaned forward and kissed her chastely on the mouth.

"Kiss me again. Stop holding back. Come on, they already think you're my fiancée. This is what engaged couples do." Faith seemed to think that little ruse had been hilarious. She'd ribbed me for it often throughout the week. "Xander, I need you to kiss me like you want me."

"Christ. Faith, I do want you. How could you even say that? Don't you realize how desperately I want to really kiss you?"

"Then why don't you?"

"Because I won't be able to stop."

"I don't want you to stop."

I chuckled. "I think the hospital staff would object if I did what I really want to do here. Besides, you're still sick. I shouldn't do things that will tire you out."

My phone rang. Faith tried to get up, but I held her in place and shifted to pry the phone out of my pocket.

"Phoenix."

"Xander! It's Sam. They got him!"

"What?"

"They found Armistead. He's been taken into custody." I had told Sam everything over lunch on Monday afternoon following my MRI.

"Where was he?"

"I'm not sure, but they picked him up on Disney property yesterday."

"That's weird," I said thoughtfully. I'd never understood why anyone would go there if they were trying to hide. Yes, there were huge crowds, but also high-tech security and facial recognition software. Possibly the worst place to go if you were trying to be invisible. As a security guard himself, he should know that. Something wasn't adding up. Where had he been? Why now?

"Yes, it is. But what a relief. Anyway, that's all I've got. How are your hands?"

I scratched at the calluses of my left hand. "Much improved. Still a little itchy."

"Any shortness of breath?"

"No. I'm good."

"When will you be up to starting practice again?"

"I'm not sure, Sam. After Faith is discharged."

Sam paused. "He can't hurt her now."

"I know."

"You promised you'd focus."

"And I will. My hands still aren't perfect, anyway. I'll get back to you, okay? Soon."

Sam grumbled something. "All right. Let me know."

The call ended and I put the phone down. "Now where were we?"

"They found Jacob?"

"Yes."

"I still don't think he did it, Xander. He wouldn't risk his career. Not for me."

"If they arrested him, I'm sure they have proof." I caressed her cheek and ran my thumb over her plump lower lip. "I love feeling your skin here. I'd missed this while you had your mask on."

She caught my thumb in her mouth and sucked, moaning. My cock instantly hardened beneath her. "Shit, Faith. Stop that."

She shifted her weight, making a point to rub against me. "Uh oh. Feels like someone is getting excited."

"Doesn't take much when you're around. Now what am I supposed to do?"

"Well—"

Her words were interrupted by a rapid knock and the door flying open.

"Can I come in?" Faith's doctor asked. Without waiting for an answer, she barged right into the room. "And how's my patient today?"

"I'm feeling much better."

"That's what we like to hear. Hop on the bed so I can listen to your lungs."

Faith uncurled to climb off my lap but I held on to her. *Shit!* She was going to get up and leave me exposed with this massive hard-on. She chuckled and pulled away again. I crossed my legs and adjusted my shirt as nonchalantly as possible.

The doctor asked Faith to cough, listening through her stethoscope. Then she looked down her throat and in her nostrils and eyes. She examined her burns which, like mine, were almost healed. The silvadene cream was good stuff.

"Well, Ms. Richardson, I'd say you've made excellent progress in the last couple of days." The doctor walked over to the monitor and pressed a few buttons. "You were on the mild end of the spectrum for carbon monoxide poisoning. You were lucky. You've shown no sign of mental difficulty. Your blood oxygen levels are looking pretty good. Not quite to where we'd like them for a non-smoker your age, but looking pretty good. Up to ninety-seven on average. Tell me about your home situation. There anyone in your house with you?"

Faith shook her head. "My parents live a few hours from here, up in Gainesville. They're off on a Mediterranean cruise thing right now. They don't even know I'm here. I'm the only one in my apartment."

"Well… I was going to discharge you today. However, I don't really want you to be unsupervised for a week or so, in case your condition worsens. Perhaps someone can stay with you? Or we can arrange a home health nurse, but it'll take a few—"

"That won't be necessary," I said. "She can stay with me."

"I wouldn't want to intrude," Faith said softly.

"Faith, don't be ridiculous. I've been staying here with you. What's the difference?"

"I guess…"

"Besides, you don't want to stand me up for our date tomorrow, do you?" I said with a wink.

Her grin could have lit up the room. "All right. I guess I do have someone with me. So I get to go home, then?"

"I see no reason why not," said the doctor.

"What about exercise? Or am I on bed rest?"

"Do you work?"

"Of course."

"Well, today is Wednesday. I don't want you to return to work until a week from Monday. You are not on bed rest, though. You can exercise, just keep it reasonable. Listen to your body. If you feel burning or irritation in your chest, stop immediately. If you start wheezing and it's uncontrolled by the rescue inhaler, come back in. If you notice your lips or fingernails turning blue, come back. If you cough up any blood… guess what I want you to do?"

"Come back?"

"See? You've got this. I'll write up the orders and you'll be free to go. Your nurse will be in soon to remove your IV."

The door shut with a *bang*. Faith's eyes glittered with mischief. "Smooth, Xander."

"Hmm?"

"With the shirt."

"Oh, like you weren't obvious with your exercise question."

"A girl's gotta keep in shape." She winked.

"That so?"

"Yep. So tell me something, Xander."

"Hmm?"

"Do you put out on the first date?"

"Faith, I–I don't know. We'll see how you're feeling."

"I feel great."

"We'll see."

Faith walked back over to me and waited, her hands on her hips. I uncrossed my legs so she could crawl back into my lap and curl up against my chest.

"I can hear your heart beating," she murmured.

"It beats for you, baby."

"That was cheesy."

"Yet you're smiling."

"Maybe I like cheesy."

I chuckled.

"What are we doing tomorrow night?"

I tapped the side of my nose. "That's for me to know and you to find out."

In truth, I hadn't really put much thought into it. All my energy had gone into worrying about her health and keeping an eye on her. I was glad she'd be staying with me; it made it easier for me to watch over her.

"Give me a hint."

"Mmm… we're going rock climbing."

"Very funny."

"I don't know, Faith. Date options are limited because I don't want to tire you out. Maybe we should just go traditional and catch a movie?"

"Fine with me. Or we can stay in and watch one."

"I'd like to take you out, unless you don't feel up to it."

"Okay. It's a plan. Now where were we before we were so rudely interrupted?" Faith grabbed my hand and kissed my fingers, sucking my pinky into her mouth. I snatched my hand away.

"We're in a hospital."

"I know where we are. I'm in a good mood."

"My little exhibitionist. Although I'd like nothing more than to accommodate you, I really don't need any tabloids hearing that we got caught having sex in a hospital room."

"Pretty sure medical staff isn't allowed to talk about their patients."

"Pretty sure I don't count as a patient anymore. Besides, you need to get better."

"I'm better!" Faith started coughing heavily. I sat her up straight and forced her head back, tilting her chin up so her airway was as straight as possible.

"Sure you are," I said when she recovered.

"I'm better. Really."

"I can tell. We'll get there, Faith. I'd just like to not kill you in the process." Another knock sounded at the door. I chuckled. "*This* is why I stopped you. Come in!"

The silence that followed puzzled me. I nudged Faith to get off my lap so I could go check the door. "Hello? Come in," she called.

The click preceding the slow creak of the door seemed louder than normal.

My eyes widened as I saw who was on the other side. I jumped to my feet, nearly knocking Faith over. "You've got balls to show your face here, Jacob."

Faith looked from Jacob to me and back again, the shock on her face so clear she almost looked like one of those over-dramatic carnival sketches.

"I wanted to see Faith."

"Well, there she is. Now you've seen her." I interposed my body between the two of them. Faith wore nothing but a hospital gown. Despite their history—or maybe because of it—I didn't like her being so exposed to him. "I got her out of that theater, no thanks to you. Speaking of that night… heard you'd been arrested. Why the fuck are you here?"

He started to say something, but snapped his mouth shut. Focusing on me, he squared his shoulders. "Brought in for questioning, actually. Then released. I had nothing to do with the fire."

"Bullshit!" I snapped.

"Xander…" Faith walked around me and placed a hand on my forearm.

I ignored her. "What the hell were you doing there, then?"

"Working. One of the regular security guys had a family emergency. The theater called my firm and they sent me." Jacob looked like he wanted to say something else, but changed tracks. "Faith, can I talk to you alone for a minute?"

"What the fuck?" I said. "Absolutely not. Anything you want to say in front of her, you can say in front of me." Did he think I was stupid? He'd threatened her the last time they'd spoken. The last time they'd been in a building together, she'd almost died. He'd get alone time with my girlfriend over my dead body.

"Xander." Faith's voice was calm. Too calm. I was ready to rip this asshole apart, but she sounded cool and collected. "It'll be fine. Please give us a minute."

"I will not. He threatened you. He threatened both of us. He knew you were in my home that day, which means he followed you or tracked you or something. Now he expects me to believe he just *happened* to be in the theater on the exact day that a fire got set off in your dressing room and landed you in the hospital? I don't fucking think so. Anything he has to say can be said with me here." I lowered my voice. "We're a team, baby. I don't want anything to happen to you."

Faith's eyes searched mine. She looked like she was going to argue, but seemed to realize I wasn't going to back down. She nodded, bringing her hand up to briefly stroke my cheek.

"Xander's right," Faith said, turning to Jacob. "We're a team. I don't mind if he hears whatever you have to say."

Jacob regarded us for a moment, a look of pain on his features. *Good.*

"Are you happy, Faith?" he asked.

"The fuck kind of question is that?" My fists clenched so tightly the knuckles ached.

"One I didn't ask you."

"Xander… you can stay, but let me speak for myself. Please." Faith turned to Jacob. "Yes, I am."

Jacob closed his eyes and inhaled sharply. He nodded once. "I'm glad. I wanted to ask where we… what I…" His eyes darted between Faith and me, once more looking uncomfortable.

Fuck's sake. Asshole tries to kill her then wants to know where things went wrong between them.

"…Faith, I told you I loved you, then you left me for another man. I deserve to know why."

"Jacob, it wasn't like that." Her voice was thick with unshed tears. She looked at me, a plea in her watery gaze.

I shook my head. Snatching her bathrobe off the foot of the bed, I thrust it at her. I walked to the room's only window and stared down at the parking lot. This was as far away as I was willing to go.

"I'm sorry," Faith said, her voice barely more than a whisper. "I didn't mean to hurt you."

"What did I do wrong? Tell me that."

Her voice broke. "You didn't do anything. I just... Xander and I... I... I love him. But that doesn't mean I don't care about you. It's just different."

Jacob heaved a big sigh. "It hurts, Faith."

"I'm sorry."

"Me, too." He paused. "The cops thought I had something to do with the fire. I want you to know I didn't. I helped the guests get out front. My mom caught wind of the fire on the news, and kept calling, so I went to see her. I decided I needed a break from life, so I called work and told them I wouldn't be available for a few days. I had no idea anyone was looking for me until security pulled me aside at Disney. I swear I had nothing to do with any of it. I wasn't even supposed to work that night."

"I never thought it was you," Faith said.

Jacob snorted. "That makes you the only one, apparently. It's okay. I'm not proud of how I reacted. I'd have probably thought it was me, too, if the roles were reversed." I turned to see Jacob watching me, a resigned look on his face. "Listen, are you going to the funeral, or will you still be here?"

"Funeral?" Faith asked.

"For... I think her name was Claire? It's on Friday."

"Claire's dead?" Faith covered her face with her hands and sunk onto the bed. I hurried to her side and wrapped my arm around her.

"Yeah. Smoke inhalation. Carbon monoxide poisoning. I'm sure *Xander* knows the details. Didn't he tell you?"

What? Me? My mind raced, trying to figure out what the fuck Jacob was talking about. *Shit! Claire must be the name of the other girl.* I hadn't brought her up to Faith yet. Hell, I hadn't even been sure what happened. Why would I have gotten her all upset over a theory?

"I'm sorry," I whispered, alarmed at the way she'd stiffened in my arms at the sound of my name.

"Um… so will you be able to make it?"

"I'll try." Faith's voice was thick, almost slurred. "I'm getting discharged soon, so I'm not sure what's happening."

"All right. Maybe I'll see you there. Take care of yourself, Faith."

"You, too."

He left, shutting the door behind him.

Faith sat in my arms, taking deep, shuddering breaths. I reached up to stroke her hair, but her raspy voice startled me.

"When, Xander?"

"When what?"

"You knew. You knew all along and you didn't tell me."

"To be honest, I only suspected."

"What does that even mean? Why didn't you tell me? You didn't hesitate to tell me and the cop all about your theories about Jacob."

Detective Bentley, the cop who had questioned me at the theater, had come on Monday evening to speak to Faith. According to him, the fire was being investigated as arson.

"I didn't want to upset you, Faith."

"Well, I'm pretty upset now!" she exclaimed. "So how is that working for you?"

"You want the story?"

"Yes!"

How could I explain that day? Bracing myself, I dove in. "I found her first. I went in after you, no thanks to your ex-boyfriend. Aside from that caring performance he just delivered, he did his level-fucking-best to stop me from looking for you. I saw what I thought was a wig on the floor and bent to grab it, only to realize it wasn't a wig, it was a girl. I didn't recognize her, but her face was so badly burned I probably wouldn't have, even if I knew her. I grabbed her to drag her out of there, but her legs were trapped. When I shifted her, though, I found you. She had apparently fallen on you when the ceiling collapsed.

"My only focus was getting you out of there. I could barely breathe. The smoke was so thick, the fire was still smoldering, and it was unbelievably hot. I remember comparing that room to Hell itself. I didn't know if either of you were alive, but the thought of losing you was unthinkable, so I grabbed you and pulled you out. We'd made it almost to the loading dock when the firemen got there. After that, things get kind of blurry. I guess I told them where to find her, but the next thing I remember with clarity was sitting on the ground outside the fire truck, an oxygen mask on my face. They were loading you up on the ambulance."

Faith still had her back to me. I wished she would look at me so I'd have some clue what she was thinking. I swallowed hard, trying to find the words.

"They had you on oxygen and rushed you away. They wouldn't let me come with you. Soon after, a fireman came out with Claire. He handed her off to the EMTs and they started CPR, then loaded her on an ambulance and left, too. That was the last I saw of her. My only clue of what happened to her was when a nurse asked me if I *was* family. Past tense. But it could have just been bad phrasing... I didn't really know."

"Why didn't you tell me? We've been here talking this whole time. Why wouldn't you mention *that*? What happened to us being a team? Isn't that what you *just* said to me?"

"I told you already, Faith. I didn't want to upset you." It was a partial truth, but there was more to it. I also didn't want to see the condemnation in her eyes. Because I hadn't saved her friend.

"Get away from me," she whispered. "How can I trust you?"

I jumped to my feet as if I'd been burned again. "Faith, I... of course you can trust me."

"Get out."

She was taking this far worse than I'd feared. I took a step back from her. I didn't want to go, but I was loathe to force myself on her. "Faith..."

"I said get out."

"I'm going. But... listen. I'm so sorry. I'm sorry I couldn't save her. I wanted to, but in the end... you were what was most important to me. I love you. I will always love you. I'm sorry I left her there. I know it was my fault."

I turned to leave, my heart heavy.

"Wait."

I paused but didn't turn around. This was it. If my luck held with Faith as it had with Lily, she'd spit in my face or do something equally horrible now. My hands shook. I crossed my arms over my chest so that she couldn't see how she'd affected me. Hard to believe that we'd been laughing and flirting only a few minutes before.

Faith sighed. "Don't go. I'm sorry I said that. Of course it isn't your fault. None of this is your fault."

"It is, Faith. And I know it. I should have tried harder to help her. At a glance I could tell she was in worse shape than you."

"Was she even alive then?"

"I don't know."

"Xander, come here. Please." She patted the bed next to her, and I sat down. She rested her head on my shoulder and took my hand. "I'm sorry I snapped at you. I just didn't handle the surprise well. Claire is… was… a good friend. I can't believe I'll never see her again. But I shouldn't have taken it out on you."

I squeezed her hand. "These last few days… I've been wondering if the reason you're alive is because she fell on top of you."

"Maybe."

"You were on your side underneath her. Her body was shielding you from the flame and smoke."

Faith shook her head. "I wish I could remember those last moments before I blacked out, but everything is so blurry." Her voice caught and she started to cry again.

"Shh… I'm here, baby." I pulled her into my arms and held her. I would never understand women. In the span of an hour, Faith had gone from seductive exhibitionist, to heartbroken, to angry and throwing me out, to loving, and finally heartbroken again. It was enough to give a guy whiplash. Yet… I cherished every moment. I could have lost Faith in the fire, but here she was. I no longer suspected Jacob. If he was lying, he had done a damned good job of it. I still didn't trust him, and I knew we'd never be friends, but I understood why the cops had let him go.

But that did beg the question…

Who *had* started the fire?

CHAPTER EIGHTEEN

The rest of the morning passed in a blur. We showered, packed up all our stuff, and received last minute discharge instructions. Before we knew it, a hospital volunteer wheeled Faith out the door while I served as pack mule.

We'd no sooner stepped out the door than I became aware of a familiar clicking sound. "There they are!" a voice shouted.

"Get Ms. Richardson back inside," I ordered in a quiet voice.

"What is going on?" the elderly female volunteer asked.

"Someone tipped off the fuc–the press. Get her back inside. I'll come around with the car."

Faith tugged on the side of my pants. "Are you sure you should–"

"Don't argue with me. Not about this. And don't touch me right now. I'll take care of everything." Without a second glance, I took off carrying all the stuff we'd had in the hospital room. I ignored the shouts of "Mr. Phoenix, can you tell me in your own words what happened at the theater?" and "Mr. Phoenix, are the rumors true that you're getting back into gymnastics? How will what happened at the theater affect that?"

I reached my car and shoved everything into the trunk. I breathed a big sigh of relief and shut the door. They hadn't followed me here, choosing for once to take a hint.

"Mr. Phoenix, is it true that Ms. Richardson is your fiancée?" My blood froze in my veins. I knew that sultry voice. Exotic. Right behind me.

I spun around to find Amara standing far closer to me than I would have liked. "Long time no see."

"And you're still as muscly as ever. Answer the question."

"I thought you were an editor now. No more interviews."

"Oh, I've taken a personal interest in this one. It's so exciting, don't you think?"

"Not really."

"Oh, I do," she purred. "This story has it all. Love, danger, excitement, betrayal, death…"

"Back off."

"Lily misses you, you know. She won't admit it, but she does."

"She's a two-faced, manipulative bitch who spread lies about me in your shit rag paper."

"You broke her heart. Are you surprised she would lash out?"

"Let's have a reality check here. *She* dumped *me*. After I proposed, no less."

"That's not her version."

"That's the truth. She could do with a lesson in what truth is, especially if she ever so much as *considers* writing one single word about me again."

"Your reappearance at the office messed her up all over again, just like when you two broke up months ago. Did you know she came crawling back to me, crying and homeless? I took her back, of course. What are friends for?"

"I couldn't care less," I hissed.

"Oh, you certainly sound like you don't care, X-Wing. That much is obvious."

"I'm done with this. You two deserve each other. What the fuck do you want from me, Amara?"

"I simply want to know if it's true what my sources say about you and Ms. Richardson."

"If I tell you, will *you* tell *me* who your sources are?"

"Can't do that, Mr. Phoenix. I'd hate for you to go after them."

"Then we are done here. Get out of my way." I stomped to the driver door and threw it open. "And I don't give a shit about Lily Campbell. Not anymore."

"Who do *you* think is behind the fire?" she yelled after me, but I jumped in the car and slammed the door shut.

I punched the ignition button and threw the car in reverse, slamming my left foot on the clutch. A glance in my mirror told me that Amara was scurrying to safety, so I backed out of the parking spot and took off for the entrance, silently daring any more reporters to be in the way. I pulled up to the front door and hopped out of the car to assist Faith.

The trip was quiet and awkward. I was still fuming about my run-in with Amara and had no way to explain what had happened. Faith seemed to sense my reticence and didn't press me. I took her home so I could help her pack her bags, then brought her to my place.

I opened her car door for her, but she hesitated. "Who was she, Xander?"

"Excuse me?"

"The girl. I saw her follow you. You seemed familiar with each other."

"If by familiar you mean I nearly strangled her in broad daylight, then yes."

"Tell me."

"She's an editor for *Celebrities and Sinners*. A tabloid. She is Lily's best friend."

"What did she want?"

"To ask stupid questions about you and try to get to me regarding Lily. One of the hospital staff leaked that I'd said you're my fiancée."

"So that's why you're so upset?"

"I don't want to talk about it."

"Oh, come on." Faith climbed out of the car and placed her hand on my cheek, stroking against the stubble. I leaned into her hand and tried to calm down. "Hey, if you're going to be my fiancé, you have to tell me everything. No secrets."

I inhaled sharply, my eyes searching hers. Was she serious? Was I ready for that? Was she? A plan was already hatching in the back of my mind, despite my reservations.

"Let's go inside." Once she was seated comfortably seated on the couch, I joined her there and pulled her against me. I'd been through hell for this woman, but right here, right now, this was our heaven.

"Are you going to tell me why you're so upset now?"

So much for heaven. "Amara was Lily's best friend. Despite that, she paid some slime to spike her drink with a date rape drug. The plan was to get pictures to blackmail her with so that Amara would beat her out for the editor position."

"Oh God, how awful. Some best friend."

"I know. When I figured it out, I asked Lily to move in with me. She was living with Amara and had no place else to go. When she left me, when she aborted our child... she went back to her, I guess. That's what Amara said."

"If that's true, they deserve each other."

"Maybe. Amara is a snake. She knew Lily and I were together, but it didn't stop her from hitting on me. I used to think Lily didn't belong at a tabloid, that she was better than them. But now I don't know. I think she was just as horrible and I was too blinded by lust to see it. Anyway, among other things, Amara told me Lily missed me."

"And how do you feel about that?"

I chuckled. "Are you my shrink now?"

"If you need one, then yes, I am."

"I was shocked, I think. And the pain of her betrayal came flooding back. And I was confused."

Faith plucked at a loose thread on her jeans. "Confused?"

"Yes, because if she hadn't left me, we would be together right now. She would be very pregnant, and maybe we would be happy. Maybe not. Only..."

"Yes?"

"Only, had that happened, I wouldn't have reconnected with you. Believe me when I tell you that what I feel for you far eclipses anything Lily and I had."

"Are you sure, Xander? She was pregnant with your baby."

"Yes, I'm sure. I felt duty-bound to her, nothing more. You... well, Faith, can I ask you something?"

"What?" Her voice sounded breathy.

I kissed the top of her head and pulled her closer to me. I couldn't see her face, but that was for the best. If I saw hesitation or fear in her expression, I would change my mind.

"I felt duty-bound to her," I repeated. "But with you, I see my entire future. I see kids and grandkids. I see us growing old together, tackling everything life throws at us... together. When I told the hospital you were my fiancée, it just felt *right*. Faith, what would you say if I asked you to marry me?"

There it was. In my head, I had envisioned waiting until our date, but the question had just flowed out of me, and I couldn't take it back now. I held perfectly still and awaited her answer.

Faith turned toward me. Her eyes met and searched mine. I saw a question in their depths. I didn't know what answers she saw in mine, but the corners of her eyes crinkled in amusement. *Shit.* I braced for the inevitable rejection.

"Are you asking me?"

"Me? No. I'm not. I haven't got a ring and we haven't even been out on a normal date yet. I'm asking–hypothetically–what you would say if I *did* ask you?"

Faith's face lit up in a huge smile that brightened the room. "Well, if you *were* asking me, I'd say… *yes,* Xander. I'd love nothing more."

"Really?"

"Really. Xander, you risked your life for me. You haven't left my side this whole last crazy week. We have a lot of details to work out and need to know each other better, but *yes.* I love you and all that stuff is just what I called it: details. I can't think of anyone who would ever be better for me than you. I'd be an idiot to say no."

I pulled her to me, my lips crashing against hers, my tongue seeking entrance. Where once I would have demanded, I now requested, meeting her halfway. She yielded without hesitation, and in a moment, my tongue was inside her mouth, stroking hers. I was so overcome by her words, so blown away by the depth of my feeling for her.

All too soon I wrenched myself away, gasping for breath. If I was winded, she certainly was. "I'm sorry!"

"Why?" Faith's voice was breathy, but she sounded okay.

"I don't want to hurt you."

"Xander, honestly. You need to stop worrying. I'm fine, I promise. The doctor said I was allowed to exercise."

"Even so…"

"I need you to fuck me."

I inhaled sharply, stunned. "I–"

"I need this. I need to feel the fireworks, the connection we felt before. Please."

I couldn't resist her if I'd wanted, and I felt exactly the same way. "You have to promise me something."

"Okay," she whispered.

"You have to promise me that if you have *any* trouble breathing, you'll tell me at once so we can stop."

She hesitated.

"Faith, I'm sorry, but this is a deal-breaker. Do you promise?"

"Yes."

I watched her, trying to decide if she would really do as she said. I knew she needed this as much as I did, needed to reconnect intimately. We had to be careful, though. I would never forgive myself if I hurt her.

I stroked her lower lip with my thumb. She rolled her lips and sucked it into her mouth. Her tongue flicked over the pad. and she bit down and sucked.

My breath caught in my throat. Her eyes glowed bright, and I almost suspected if the lights were off I would still be able to make out their radiance. I was captivated, caught in her spell.

She moaned, and the vibrations danced in the tip of my thumb and sent my imagination into overdrive. My cock throbbed, begging to be buried inside her warmth. I had intended to seduce her, but within seconds she had seduced me.

I yanked my thumb away and ripped off my clothes, noticing she did the same with equal enthusiasm.

I ached for her touch. After almost losing her, after becoming so close this week, and now after she'd agreed to be mine... I needed her, needed to feel she was real.

I laid down on my back and placed my hand around the base of my cock. A bead of pre-come had already squeezed its way out and glistened on the tip.

"Get down here. I want to feel your mouth on me, doing what you just did to my finger." She dropped down to kneel beside me, but before she could touch me I sat up and grabbed her. "No. Not like that. I need to taste you." I patted my chest. "Climb on."

Faith blushed brighter than her hair. She dropped her gaze, but dutifully did what I ordered. As her leg passed over me, I could see her perfect cunt, the folds already opening to me. *Fuck me.* She was already dripping wet, her pussy lips swollen with need. I reached up and lifted her back onto my face, hooking my arms around her legs, anxious to bury my tongue inside her.

Her long fingers wrapped around my cock and squeezed. I felt her hot breath on me. Her tongue flicked out to lick just the tip as her other hand toyed with my balls. It almost tickled.

Leaning forward, I licked from her cunt up to her clit. I swirled my tongue around it, then licked back to her pussy and inside her.

She groaned and swallowed me, allowing my cock to hit the back of her throat.

"Holy *shit.*" My head fell back against the plush carpeting as I absorbed the unexpected sensation. She hadn't warmed up to that at all, just shoved her tonsils right onto my dick. "Jesus, Faith."

I went back to devouring her pussy. I moaned as her sweet juices filled my mouth. Pulling back and gripping her thighs tighter, I plunged my fingers deep inside and finger fucked her.

She let out a garbled cry as she sucked me. Her head bobbed up and down while one hand massaged my balls. Her hand rubbed and stroked lower, then pressed firmly underneath them at the same moment she deep-throated me again.

I couldn't help myself. I thrust my hips upward to meet her, barely able to concentrate enough to continue pleasuring her.

Pressing my thumb against her clit, I massaged in gentle circles while I licked and sucked at her entrance. My tongue lapped at her, reveled in her. I had always loved eating pussy, but hers was something special. Everything about her—the way she tasted, the way she felt and sounded, even her *scent*—drove me wild. I flicked my tongue rapidly, increasing the speed of my thumb on her clit to match.

Her breathing increased; I both felt and heard her gasping. She took her mouth off me and jerked me off. My concern for her mounted, even as I was growing closer and closer to orgasm. She'd promised… and I had to trust her to tell me if she needed to stop.

With a shudder, her legs tightened around my head and she ground her hips against my face. She groaned loudly as she gave in to the sensations. Her pussy contracted and tightened around my tongue, and I licked her with ever faster and firmer strokes, lengthening her pleasure as more of her juices leaked into my mouth.

Then her mouth was on me again, her fist still tight around my base. She was lost in her own orgasm but continued to work me with abandon. I was so close, and seeing her lose control from this angle while being surprised by her mouth on me was almost enough to push me over the edge. Her teeth scratched lightly over my shaft as she bobbed up and down, then she let go and plunged down, taking in as much of me as she could.

"Oh, fuck! *Faith!*" I breathed as I let go and found my own release. My hips involuntarily thrust forward with each pulse, and she swallowed every drop until I had nothing left.

She laid her head down on my leg and relaxed, still breathing heavily.

"Are you okay?" I panted.

She nodded and kissed the crease of my thigh, but otherwise didn't move.

"Hey…" I slid her leg over and off my chest and pulled her backwards until we were lying down together on the floor. "Are you sure you're okay? How's your chest?"

"I'm fine, Xander. I promise. Stop worrying."

I smoothed her hair from her face and tucked it behind her ear. "Do you know how beautiful you are? I am one lucky bastard."

Faith giggled and stroked her fingers over my chest and around my nipples. I grabbed her hand

and brought it to my mouth for a kiss. "Better stop that."

"I like touching you."

"Mmm… and I like you touching me, but I shouldn't push my luck. I need to get you settled, then I have to run a couple of errands. If you keep doing that, we'll never get anywhere."

"What kind of errands?"

"I need to head to the pharmacy for your prescriptions, and I need to talk to Sam." I also wanted to run out to the jewelry store, but I didn't want to mention that. I still had Lily's ring upstairs in my medicine cabinet, but the thought of giving it to Faith made my skin crawl. I thought I had seen that the store would do exchanges or store credit, so I was going to check it out.

"I can come with you to the pharmacy. We can stop and pick up my car."

"We'll get it later, okay? I promise. You should rest for now."

"I'm fine. I've done nothing *but* rest for the last week. I want to get my car."

It was all I could do not to laugh at her pouty tone. I kissed the top of her head. "I said no. I'll take you tonight if you still feel up to it. I insist you rest now."

I stood and helped her to her feet, and we both put our clothes back on. "Do you think you'll be okay with the stairs? We can move into the guest bedroom for a few days if you think it would be easier."

She shot me an exasperated look. "How many times do I have to tell you I'm fine? Upstairs will be perfect. You know, it really would make much more sense to take me to get my car on the way back. You aren't supposed to leave me on my own, remember? What if something happens?"

"Thought you were fine."

"Oh, I am. You just don't seem to believe me. Makes sense to continue to err on the side of caution, don't you think?"

"Nice try. If I shouldn't leave you home alone, what makes you think you should be driving? I'll ask Sam to help me pick up your car." I gestured for Faith to proceed me up the stairs. I noticed my bedroom door was closed as soon as we hit the landing.

I always kept it open, whether I was in there or downstairs or out of the house. It helped with air circulation, because my room was always the warmest.

Well... Sam did come in to find some clothes for me. He probably shut it.

"Faith, hold up. Let me grab that door for you."

She sighed. "I've got it."

"Wait, but—"

Faith flung open the door and barged in. I followed quickly behind her, frowning.

"What happened in here?" she demanded.

The bedsheets were torn off the mattress and lay in a messy pile. All the drawers were open, including my bedside table. The floor was littered with wadded up clothes, with more bunched up haphazardly inside the open drawers.

Someone had been searching for something.

Sam wouldn't have done this. My hands clenched into fists as my mind raced to every possible conclusion, dismissing them all. I whipped my phone out of my pocket and tapped the screen.

"Hello?"

"Sam, the fuck you do to my room?"

"What?" My heart sank at the confusion in his voice.

"The entire bedroom's been tossed. Someone stripped the bed, went through the drawers. There's shit everywhere."

"Well, it wasn't me, Xander. Was your door broken? Any sign of forced entry? Any idea what they were after?"

"Nothing looked out of place downstairs. Door was locked. Didn't check the door to the gym. What the hell, man?"

"Should I come down there?"

"No. I'll call you later. We have something else we need to discuss, anyway. But not now." Without waiting for his answer, I terminated the call.

I looked in my bedside table. The box of condoms had been ripped apart as if an animal had gotten to them. The foil packages had been ripped open, and the rubbers were scattered everywhere. Strange. Even stranger, the living room had shown no sign of trespass. Nothing had been touched. The television, stereo, and other electronics had all been exactly where I'd left them.

"Should we call the police?" Faith sounded as nervous and confused as I felt.

"I don't want them in my house. The ambulance chasers always follow."

"What?"

I chuckled darkly. "The press. Haven't you heard that term? You almost were one."

"Xander, focus. Someone broke into your house and went through your things. They could have taken God only knows what. You need to have them come investigate."

Fuck it. I knew she was right, but I really didn't want to make the call. I surveyed the disaster that was my bedroom. Someone had been in here. Someone had been looking for something. In *my* home. I felt exposed, violated. What had they wanted?

"What else do you have here? Electronics? Jewelry? Xander, where are your medals?"

"In my gym." My blood ran cold as a thought occurred to me. "One second."

I walked into my bathroom and yanked open the medicine cabinet. Nothing in here appeared to be messed with, but you never knew. I withdrew a small bag from the bottom shelf. Inside were a couple of tubes of liniment that I had brought home from the hospital following my back injury. At the very bottom was a small black box. I grabbed it, dropping the bag on the counter, and flicked it open.

I breathed a sigh of relief as the sparkling diamond caught the fluorescent lighting. This was the only jewelry of any real value in my house. Lily's engagement ring. I had all but forgotten about it after she… wait…

Did I get the key back from Lily?

Chapter Nineteen

What the actual fuck?

I thought back to that night before the fire. I had been so sure someone had been in my house, but I hadn't been able to find anyone. Was it possible Lily could have been coming in here? What did she want?

"What are you doing?" Faith asked.

I snapped the box closed and slipped it into my pocket. "Nothing. Let's go check downstairs."

Nothing in the guest room looked out of place, which puzzled me. If it was Lily, why would she rifle through *my* stuff? *This* had been her room. It would make sense that if she were looking for something, this is where she'd look.

I threw open the doors to my gym and did an extensive search, Faith close behind. My medals were all where I'd left them, all my equipment looked untouched, and the back door was bolted shut.

I checked the time on my phone. Only a little after three. With a frustrated groan, I pulled up my internet browser and searched for *Celebrities and Sinners'* phone number.

"Are you calling the police now?"

I shook my head and held a finger up to my lips. The line clicked open.

"Celebrities and Sinner's office, Brittany speaking. How may I direct your call?"

I cleared my throat. "Lily Campbell, please."

"I'm sorry, but Ms. Campbell has been out sick on medical leave. I'm not sure when she'll return."

Your reappearance at the office messed her up all over again, just like when you two broke up months ago. That's what Amara had said. Seemed Lily was even more fucked up than I'd thought. "Fine. Let me speak to Amara, then. I can't remember her last name, but she's an editor."

"I'm sorry, but she's away from her desk. Would you like me to put you through to her voicemail?"

"You don't happen to have her cell number, do you? It's urgent."

Brittany paused. "And you are...?"

"My name is Alexander Phoenix. She was working on an article and had some questions for me."

"Oh! Yes, Mr. Phoenix. Let me get that for you."

Brittany gave me the number, and I ended the call.

"What does your ex have to do with anything?" Faith asked.

"I'm not sure she does, but I'm going to find out. Why don't you go sit on the couch? I'll come with you."

I punched in the number and waited while it rang.

"Hello?"

"Amara?"

"Yes...?"

"It's Xander."

"Mr. Phoenix, is that really you?" I could practically hear her self-satisfied grin. "I'm honored."

"Cut the crap, Amara."

"What can I do for you?"

"Where's Lily?" Faith's head snapped around to stare at me, but I pretended not to notice.

"She's been, um, sick lately, so I expect she's at home. Why do you ask?"

"I need her number."

"Do you now?" purred Amara.

"Don't make me ask twice."

"Well, isn't this an interesting situation? I have something you want, and you... ahh... you always have something I want."

"What's that?"

"I want an interview with you and Ms. Richardson."

"Not a chance. You stay away from Faith. She has nothing to do with you. I mean it, Amara."

"Then I'm afraid I can't help you. I seem to have lost Lily's number."

"Fuck this shit. Just tell her to stay the hell out of my home. Let her know I'm changing the locks. She can keep that key as a memento." I disconnected the call, beyond furious and wishing I had the option to slam the phone down. Hitting "end call" was nowhere near as satisfying.

"Xander…"

"Don't." I struggled to keep myself in control. The last thing I wanted was to freak out on Faith.

"You think Lily's behind this?"

"She changed her number the very day she left me. I never got the key back, never thought of it. Lily, Sam, and I are the only ones with keys, and I see no sign of forced entry. I just don't understand *why*."

"I still think you should call the cops. Even with a key, she doesn't have the right to just enter your house."

"I gave her a key willingly, and she didn't steal anything that I can tell. I don't think they would call it a crime."

"You don't know it was her."

"Who else could it be?" I demanded.

"And what does Amara have to do with any of this?"

"She is apparently my only link to Lily."

"I'll talk to her, then."

"*Absolutely not.*"

"We'll meet in public and I'll answer her questions. What could it possibly hurt? I don't care if she writes horrible things about me in her stupid tabloid. No one reads those things anyway."

"My answer is no, and that is final." I looked up a locksmith and made an emergency service call, then called Sam. I didn't want to leave Faith by herself.

But I needed to get out for a bit.

Chapter Twenty

Faith had been behaving strangely since last night.

Sam had come over and we discussed training again. Leaving him with Faith, I'd gone to the pharmacy and to the jewelry store to exchange the ring. Lily's ring had been a gaudy princess cut design, while Faith's was more of a classical solitaire look with an oval-shaped diamond. Baguettes sparkled on either side of the stone, and the moment I had seen it I knew it had been made for Faith.

The locks had been changed, and I gave a key to Sam and Faith, with a spare that I kept in the kitchen drawer. I'd confessed to Sam that I intended to propose to Faith. He shook his head but didn't seem surprised. He didn't complain, either.

After he left, Faith and I set out to get her car, but first we stopped at a phone store to buy her a replacement, as hers had been destroyed in the fire. New phone in hand, with orders to call me immediately if she felt unwell, we returned home and made dinner before cleaning up everything in the bedroom. She'd seemed distant, distracted. But I assumed it was because of all that had happened.

I had made long, slow love to her in my bed, and we fell asleep in each other's arms. She'd seemed better then, so I felt reassured.

Faith was back to acting weird this morning over breakfast. Skittish or nervous, even. I had no idea why but had resolved to address it later today.

Sam had been pleased with my performance during practice. Faith hadn't come in to watch, and I wasn't sure what she'd been up to, but I had devoted all my energy to my routines, to pushing my body to reach and exceed our goals.

"Great job today, hotshot. Keep it up."

"See you tomorrow." I shut the door behind Sam and hopped up the stairs to find Faith.

I strolled into the room, but instead of finding my beautiful soon-to-be fiancée, I found the bed made and a note on a bedside table.

Xander,

I'll be out for the next couple of hours or so. Please don't worry. I'll be back soon. And don't be angry, it's for you.

Love,

Your Faith

What was that supposed to mean? I knew I shouldn't have taken her to get her car. I turned on the shower and grabbed my phone to call her while it heated up.

"Xander?" Faith's voice was breathy, as if she were trying to keep quiet.

"Where did you go?"

"Out to lunch with a friend. I'll be back soon."

"Wait, the X-Wing doesn't know you're here with me?" The deep, sultry voice in the background was annoyingly familiar. I fought down the rage.

"Tell Amara I said hello." My voice was quiet. Much quieter than usual. It took all my restraint to not fly off the handle.

"Are you angry with me?"

Fuck yeah! "What do you think?"

"I'm sorry."

"Are you?"

"No."

"Why say it then?"

"Because I don't want you to be angry. We're almost done here, so I'll talk to you soon. I love you."

I hung up, unable to answer. I clenched my hands into fists to stop them from shaking. Shower. I needed to take a shower. Maybe that would calm me down. No, not enough. I shut off the water and stomped back down the stairs. I was going back to my gym. Maybe some free weights would do the trick.

I moved the weights into the center of the room so I could watch the front door and got started. Half an hour into my sets, I gave up and moved to the treadmill.

I lost all sense of time after I hit my stride. I ran and ran. Was I running from my problems or chasing them? Hard to say. Was it so unreasonable that I didn't want Faith to have anything to do with my ex or anyone close to her? I didn't think so. I knew she thought she was doing the right thing, but she needed to understand that she had crossed the line.

The sound of the door opening wrenched me from my thoughts. I stepped off the treadmill and stood in the center of the room, arms crossed. Faith stared at me from the door, looking dumbfounded, as if she hadn't expected I would be awaiting her return.

She drew closer, moving slowly, cautiously.

"How was lunch?" My voice was cold, harsher than I'd intended it to be.

"Interesting." Faith whispered, clearly nervous.

"And what did Amara want?"

"She just asked me some questions. About me, about you. Your family. *Us.*"

"My family?" My mouth went dry. I knew it was stupid, knew Amara had already heard all of my so-called secrets, but my knee-jerk reaction still slammed into me just the same.

"Yes, but I told her you didn't like to talk about your family and had always shot me down when I asked."

Relief flooded through me. "What was all this about?"

"I don't know. She said she wanted an interview when I talked to her on the phone this morning, but she didn't take any notes. She was friendly and professional. She told me she knew she'd made some big mistakes in the past and that she knew you and Lily had paid for them. It almost seemed like just chatting with a girlfriend."

"'Big mistakes' is an understatement. Amara is not your *friend*. I'm not even sure she understands the meaning of the word. She risked her *friend's* life over a *promotion*."

"She regrets that. Look, I know how to handle reporters, okay? Besides, she seemed nice."

"*Nice?* Amara is a lot of things, but *nice* isn't one of them. She can't be trusted. She's dirty and underhanded and I can't fucking *believe* you went behind my back that way!"

"She didn't seem like she was fishing for a negative story. I don't know, Xander. She was nice!"

"Sure. Nice… and going to plaster my picture all over her shit rag tabloid. It doesn't matter what you told her, it doesn't matter what you gave her, it doesn't matter what she asked. All that matters to her is selling her story and making me uncomfortable. I'd sworn to sue if they even *thought* about writing anything about me again without verifying every single word was one hundred percent true, and you've offered her information on a silver platter. You were her pawn. And did you even stop to think about me? About how this would affect me? Jesus, Faith, I can't believe you'd be so stupid."

She glared at me, flames flickering in her eyes. All regret vanished from her tone and stance. All that was left was fury. "Stupid? *That's* what you think of me? Fuck you, Xander!"

I scowled and stepped closer to her. She turned away, so I grabbed her shoulders and forced her to look at me. "God damn it, Faith. No. I don't think you're stupid. Just the opposite. But I do think you should have used that head of yours before sneaking out of here behind my back and spilling your guts to a fucking reporter. *Especially* that one."

"You don't know that she'll write anything bad! She told me she's wanted to do an interview with you since the first time she met you. But do you really think I went there just to give her a scoop? I got your damned phone number, Xander."

"What are you talking about?"

"Yeah, Lily's number. I got it for you. What I don't understand is why you're so overbearing. You think you always have to be the one calling the shots. I'm not a damsel in distress. I don't *need* your protection. I didn't need it at the game store with Mark. I didn't need it with Jacob. And I *certainly* didn't need your protection to handle Amara. I can handle myself around reporters and anyone else. Why can't you just *trust* me?" She slapped the flat of her hand into my sweaty chest, making a loud sound as if to enunciate her point.

"Fuck…" It was all I could do to whisper the single word before we were on each other. My hand tangled in her hair and I pulled her head back, forcing her mouth up to meet mine. She gasped, and I took advantage of that fact to thrust my tongue into her mouth. All the fight went out of me, tamed by the woman I loved.

She pulled away, breathing hard. "I'm not sorry I went. I *am* sorry that I hurt you."

I sat on the floor, tugging her down to join me. "I *do* trust you, Faith. I trust you more than I've ever trusted anyone, except for Sam. Maybe."

"You have a funny way of showing it."

"Look. I'm sorry, too. This relationship stuff is new for me. I don't think you're a damsel in distress. I think you are an intelligent, capable woman. That said, it pisses me off that you went behind my back. We have to learn to be a team."

"I want that, too." She leaned back against my chest, reaching up to stroke my ear. "Are you going to call her?"

"Who?"

"Your ex."

"As soon as I figure out what to say."

"You didn't hesitate yesterday."

"Yesterday, I was crazy pissed and probably would have said something stupid. Today, still pissed, but more rational."

"I still think you should have called the cops. She's stalking you. She followed you to the theater, too."

I paused. "How did you know that?"

"Amara mentioned it. Wait, you knew?"

"An article I saw online had a picture of us. I saw her in the background, but I hadn't seen her there that night. What else did Amara say?"

"Nothing much. She just told me I should be careful because you use women and throw them away." Faith looked away. I said nothing, watching her impassively. "She said Lily saw you ordering food at the theater and just the sight upset her so much she stayed in bed for two days."

"I didn't use Lily, and I certainly didn't throw her away. *She* left *me*... wait. Did you say she saw me ordering food?"

"Yes. Before the fire, I guess. Why?"

I stood, holding out a hand to help Faith off the floor. "Come upstairs. I have to check something."

I jerked the bedside table drawer open, then grabbed my laptop out and powered it on. Pulling up the internet browser, I searched the theater's name. Just as I had seen before, there was the article about the fire. I clicked on the picture where Lily was shown and enlarged it, then enlarged it some more.

It was definitely her, standing at an angle to the camera, out on the loading dock. Again I wondered how I hadn't seen her before. She wasn't dressed for a night at a dinner theater. It looked like she was wearing jeans and a t-shirt. It stood to reason that a reporter being called to the scene of a fire may not be in business attire, but it *didn't* make sense that she would have seen me ahead of time. It also didn't make sense that she wore a black shirt that said "ROA" on the back. The guy that brought me backstage the first time wore a black roadie t-shirt. This was obviously an identical one.

But Lily wasn't a roadie.

Why was she there?

I couldn't see her right hand in the picture, but her left hand was empty. No note pad. No photographer with her. I enlarged the picture again.

Her left hand was in shadow, or covered in dirt or soot. I couldn't tell which because of the photo's low resolution. Her jeans also had the same dark spots on them. The fire had been localized to the dressing room and the attic above it. There was no real reason for her to be covered in soot.

"Holy shit, Lily. What did you do?" I grabbed my phone. "I need that phone number, Faith."

"What's going on?"

She handed me a slip of paper. I gestured to the screen as I punched in the number.

"Hello?"

"Lily?"

Silence. I checked my phone to make sure she hadn't hung up. The call timer ticked away. "Lily?"

"Yes?" She sounded funny, as if she were crying. Or high. Or both.

"Been a while."

"Yes." She sniffled. That answered that; definitely crying. Faith frowned and looked like she wanted to say something. I held my finger to my lips.

"Did you find what you were looking for here?" I began to pace.

"I didn't take anything," she whispered. I had to be careful. I didn't want her to hang up. Not yet.

"I know. You still shouldn't have come. I've changed the locks."

"Xander?"

"What?"

"I'm sorry about everything. I'm sorry we fought. I'm sorry I wrote that article. I'm sorry I didn't accept your ring. I know that was wrong. I could tell it cost you a ton of money, and I was wrong to throw it back in your face. It was sweet of you to ask me, and I hope the jeweler was able to take it back."

I gritted my teeth. "Never mind all that. Why didn't you come say hello at the theater?"

"Where?"

"At the theater last Friday. I heard you had gotten a job there."

Lily laughed, a hollow, manic sound. "I work at *CaS*. You know that. Remember? You found me there and made a horrible and embarrassing scene.

I almost called security. But yeah, I work there, not at any theater. You heard wrong."

"Really? I thought I saw you."

"Just one of those faces."

"That must be it." I thought back to the bar and the time I had said those exact words to her. She had pretended she didn't recognize me, and I had stupidly fallen for her act. A white lie, maybe. But that was only the beginning. Soon she was hiding big things from me, one lie snowballing into another.

"What would you say if I told you I had a picture of you there wearing a roadie shirt?"

"What? Um, I'd say you must be mistaking me for someone else. I stayed home that night."

"Cut the shit, Lily. You were there. Why lie about it?"

Lily sobbed into the phone. "I never worked there! Check the employment records. You won't find me. I stayed home that night, Xander. I've stayed home a *lot* recently, and written from home."

I went back to the computer and examined the screen. No, I *knew* it was her. Opening another tab, I searched for the *Celebrities and Sinners* article about the fire. *Got you now.* "Who covered the fire from *CaS*?"

She didn't answer. I waited, letting the awkward silence build.

"I–I did."

"I know. I'm looking at the article right now. *Demon Barber brings Fire and Brimstone,* by Lily A. Campbell. Your own byline. You must be very proud. Even if it is for a shit tabloid and has a shittier, misleading title. Good article, though. Very detailed. In fact… tell me, Lily. How did you manage to make this article sound so detailed if *you weren't there?*"

"I don't–"

"Don't lie to me. You're in the picture. That puts you there. And your pal Amara said you'd seen me before the fire even started. So do you want to start telling the truth? No more fucking lies, Lily. I know what you did. But I can't understand why."

The sound of the sobbing abruptly stopped as the line went dead.

"Do you remember the police detective's name that visited us in the hospital?" I asked Faith as I started digging through my drawer looking for his card.

"Bentley."

"That's it."

"What's it?"

"I need his number. I know what happened."

"Tell me." Faith pulled a business card out of her purse and handed it to me.

I dialed the number. "Hello, Detective Bentley? This is Xander Phoenix."

CHAPTER TWENTY-ONE

"You were right about that one. She is one sick puppy," Detective Bentley said.

So much for date night. After I called the police and told them everything I knew, including my observations on the picture, they had sent someone out to bring Lily in for questioning. Now Faith and I sat here in the detective's office.

"I'd never had that impression before," I said sadly.

"Well, she is. After what we found at her apartment, I don't think she'll be leaving us for quite some time."

"What was there?"

"Mostly, things about you. Newspaper clippings detailing the fire and every article I think anyone has ever written about your career. Articles from magazines, so many pictures. She had a full obsession going on. There were also pictures of Ms. Richardson and some not-so-flattering caricatures. She kept a journal, too. Just what we found in there would be enough to convict."

"Oh God."

"Seems she blamed you for the loss of her career and the loss of her child, Mr. Phoenix. Care to elaborate on what happened?"

"She told me she was pregnant. Biggest shock of my life. Almost lost my career over it. I proposed, she rejected me and had an abortion. Simple as that."

"That's not her version."

"Well, that's what happened."

"I'm just telling you so you know. She claims you left her alone, and that's why she ended it. I think she was feeling resentful. Blamed you for everything."

I shook my head. "I did leave after she told me. I just needed time to think. Why would she have pictures of Faith?"

"I think…" started Faith. "She was probably just mad at you for moving on first."

"That's no reason to turn into a homicidal lunatic."

"I kind of feel bad for her. From what you told me, she lost her best friend, lost her boyfriend, quit her job, lost her baby, and lost her home… all within a few months."

"She killed her baby," I corrected.

"And maybe she regretted that. Just one more thing to be resentful for."

"I think Ms. Richardson is right," Bentley said. "Smart woman you've got there."

"No," I said. "I still don't understand. If I'm such a horrible person, why wouldn't she just come after me? Why hurt Faith? Why the theater? A woman she didn't even know ended up dead."

"She attacked me…" Faith said, "because… because she knew that would hurt you more than going after you directly. Plus, if she was really obsessed with you, she was probably harboring hope she would get you back at some point."

"I don't know…" I remembered the ring on her finger when I had confronted her at *CaS.* She had hidden it from me.

I'm sorry I didn't accept your ring…

Oh my God… was that *what she'd been looking for all that time? The engagement ring? Why?*

"Do you deny that it would hurt you more?"

"No, but we had been together less than a day. How would she know?"

Bentley cleared his throat. "She had lots of pictures of the two of you together, mostly taken at night. Outside a house and in a restaurant."

"She was following us?" I stared at him, becoming more shocked by the moment.

"Undoubtedly."

"She would have had opportunity to see us together for weeks," Faith said.

"How did I never see her?"

No one answered. I didn't really expect them to.

"*Damn it.* All that time, she was right under our noses, and I never noticed. Not once. This means she wrote that article when she did to try to scare you away, Faith. On the phone, she commented that she was sorry she'd rejected my ring. Now I wonder if *that's* what she was after the entire time." I slapped my palm on the desk. The level she had stooped to stunned me. I had once thought of Lily as being a sweet girl with manipulative friends who should have never been working at a tabloid. I was clearly wrong. She was cut from the same cloth as Amara. Her so-called best friend may have told Faith that she felt remorse over her crimes, but it didn't change the fact that she still drugged Lily without hesitation. Amara could have killed Lily… and Lily *did* kill Claire. They both needed professional help.

A cool hand rubbed at the back of my neck, Faith's nails scratching my scalp. "It's over, now. Don't blame yourself."

"I wish I'd never met her. None of this would have happened."

"You don't know that." Faith squeezed the back of my neck one final time, then addressed Bentley. "Did you have any other questions for us?"

"No, but I'll let you know if we think of any more. You're free to go."

"What will happen to her now?" I asked.

"That's up to the courts to decide, Mr. Phoenix. A lot of the evidence regarding the fire is circumspect, but she does have a motive. We've reached out to the photographer who took the picture to get a copy of the original. I suspect that will help. We're also going to check surveillance again from the surrounding buildings to look for her."

I nodded. It was all out of our hands. Whatever Lily's fate held in store, I just hoped I never had to lay eyes on her again.

We shook hands with Detective Bentley and left the station. The humid air hit us the moment we had stepped into the balmy Florida summer.

"It's a bit late for a movie, but would you like to go out for dinner?" I said.

"Sure. What did you have in mind?"

That's a good question. The small ring box in my pocket pressed into my thigh when I opened her door. Inspiration struck.

A smile tugged at my lips. "How about Mexican?"

EPILOGUE

Two years later…

Power.
Strength.
Control.

These were the attributes I valued, lived by. They had become my mantra.

My body was an extension of my mind. If I could imagine it, I could do it. Nothing would stop me from reaching my goals.

My arms and abdominals strained. My spine was held upright, with my legs parallel to the ground as if I were sitting… except I was nearly ten feet in the air, suspending my full weight from two rings hanging from the ceiling. I counted in silence, forcing my face to remain impassive. I refused to make a single sound.

I extended my legs farther in front of me and lifted slowly into a handstand. I held that position for a few seconds, then lowered myself down into an Iron Cross. Only one thing left to do…

I raised back into a handstand and started to spin. Two revolutions, then release. I curled in on myself, tumbled three times, and landed. *Perfect!*

The crowd went wild as I stuck the landing and straightened, throwing my arms up in the air in triumph. I couldn't stop my grin if I'd wanted to.

"And that's a strong performance from Alexander Phoenix," said the announcer. "Waiting to see what the judges think of that!"

I strode off the competition mat to the sound of the announcer being repeated in several other languages. Faith waddled over to me as I hit the bench area. She was in her second trimester. Her face glowed with the same pride that I knew covered my face. I threw my arms around her and tipped her back in my arms, kissing her passionately.

"Yeah! Great job, hotshot," Sam yelled over the crowd and slapped me on the back.

"Couldn't have done it without you, old man."

"You bet your ass you couldn't!" Sam said with a laugh.

To think I had almost lost everything a couple of years ago. A back injury, a rejected engagement, and a psycho ex that burned down an entire building. Back then, I'd never imagined that such a comeback was possible.

The day I'd married Faith had truly been the best day of my life. She'd never looked so beautiful.

Sam and I had worked hard getting me back into condition. Three months after Faith and I announced our engagement, though, the sponsors had refused to even consider funding a trip to the next qualifier. I'd been sure it meant the end, but an impassioned speech from Sam had made enough of them reconsider. A week later, he got the approval call and I boarded a plane for Sweden.

Hard work and determination had seen me through. I'd claimed the top spot at every qualifier I competed in, but I'd missed so many I was still doubtful that I would have a shot.

I had missed making the Olympic team on rings by a mere five points, but was named as an alternate. That brought Faith and me here to Brazil.

Unfortunately, one of the team members had ended up with the flu and then pneumonia, so I had stepped up in his place.

Whether I won or lost in these Olympic Games, it didn't matter. I'd proven a comeback was possible. I had shown the country what I was made of and, in that moment, I felt like the luckiest man in the entire world.

And Lily? She had pled guilty to arson at the recommendation of her lawyer. He had argued temporary insanity and had gotten her second degree murder charge dropped to involuntary manslaughter. She was still in prison, but was receiving regular counseling.

"X-Wing! X-Wing! X-Wing!" I realized the crowd was chanting. I stood and spread my arms to them as I waited for the results of my rings event.

The scoreboard lit up.

$$7.8 + 9.3 = 17.1$$

The crowd screamed. That placed me firmly in the lead. I waved to the crowd and punched the air in victory, then sat down next to my wife to watch my competitors. It was still anyone's game. China, in particular, always excelled in gymnastics, but I hadn't made it easy for them and was thrilled with that score.

I grabbed Faith's hand and kissed her fingers.

Game on, world, I'm back!

The end.

ABOUT THE AUTHOR

David S. Scott is a new author of erotica and erotic romance novels. After fishing his debut novels, *Deep in You* and its sequel *Deeper in You*, he is moving on to several other projects, including an erotic paranormal tentatively titled *Obsidian Angel*. He is in his mid-thirties and happily married, and has a bit of a wicked sense of humor. When not writing, David can be found reading a variety of genres or playing "nerd games" like Dungeons and Dragons with his friends. David loves interacting with people and meeting new friends, so please be sure to follow him on his author page:

https://www.facebook.com/AuthorDavidScott

www.ingramcontent.com/pod-product-compliance
Lightning Source LLC
Chambersburg PA
CBHW021236250626
47155CB00008B/3042